Amy McDougall, Master Matchmaker

Gary Pedler

Fitzroy Books

Published by Fitzroy Books
An imprint of
Regal House Publishing, LLC
Raleigh, NC 27612
All rights reserved

https://fitzroybooks.com

Printed in the United States of America

ISBN -13 (paperback): 9781646030637
ISBN -13 (hardcover): 9781646031146
ISBN -13 (epub): 9781646030880
Library of Congress Control Number: 2020941037

All efforts were made to determine the copyright holders and obtain their permissions in any circumstance where copyrighted material was used. The publisher apologizes if any errors were made during this process, or if any omissions occurred. If noted, please contact the publisher and all efforts will be made to incorporate permissions in future editions.

Interior and cover design by Lafayette & Greene
lafayetteandgreene.com
Cover images © by C.B. Royal

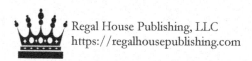 Regal House Publishing, LLC
https://regalhousepublishing.com

Author image © Mary Muszynski
Printed in the United States of America

To my parents
who gave me so much

Contents

Chapter 1

It was only the second day the photo exhibit had been open. The rooms were packed.

I'd been to a few exhibits like this before with Dad, and I thought I knew what people were supposed to do there.

Look at a photo of, say, a headless doll in a wheelbarrow.

Make some comment to the person they were with. Like, "Clearly the doll symbolizes life." Or death, or life after death, or life without death, or whatever.

Then move on to another photo.

But no. Watching the people milling through the exhibit, I saw that most of them did something else. As they walked toward the next photo, they'd swivel their heads, taking a gander at the other visitors.

"Everyone is looking at each other," I half-whispered to Dad.

"Of course they are," he half-whispered back.

It was because of Dad that we were spending Sunday afternoon in the San Francisco Museum of Modern Art. Dad was a photographer and totally nutcase about photos. Me, I liked photos so-so. My big love was drawing. As usual, I was carrying my sketchbook in my paisley-print shoulder bag, because I never knew when inspiration might strike.

"I don't get it," I said. "I thought we came here to see the photos by the Polish dude." I couldn't pronounce the name of the famous photographer. As far as I was concerned, he was just "the Polish dude."

"You don't come to a museum just to look at the art, Amy,"

Dad said. "You also come to check out the other people who are there checking out the art."

We'd stopped in front of a photo of a woman in a nightgown. She stood in an empty room with her long hair completely covering her face. Clearly she symbolized... Oh, who cared? I was more interested in understanding what Dad was saying.

"Why?" I asked.

Dad shrugged. "To find out what people are wearing. Who they're with. Whether you'd like to know them. And are they looking back at you and maybe wondering the same things."

I could make a good guess why some people were checking me out. They were giving me that look that said, "What's this Blatina chick doing with a blue-eyed white guy more than twice her age?"

I'd been getting that same look for years whenever I went out with Dad. Sometimes I wanted to wear a T-shirt that just spelled out the whole thing.

MY NAME IS AMY

I'M ADOPTED

THIS IS TRAVIS WHO ADOPTED ME

AND WHO ARE YOU?

At thirteen, I was old enough to guess why some people were giving Dad the eye. Because he was husky and handsome and late thirties. Those looks said, "Hey, you're cute, and maybe you think I am too."

I was pretty sure I got one of those looks myself. It came from a guy a year or two older than me who was there with his parents. Skinny, with red acne on his cheeks.

I looked back at the guy. In a flash, I second-guessed everything I'd chosen to wear—my black sneakers, my blue jeggings, my white stretchy top. And how did my hair look? Planned messy, or just plain old messy?

After a few tense seconds, I looked away from the guy, like I wasn't crazy about what I'd seen. Really it was more that I was embarrassed. I was sure I'd do something weird if I kept up our eye-lock any longer. Laugh, or make a face.

A minute later, I sneaked another glance at the guy. He seemed annoyed, his acne even redder than before. Probably he hadn't enjoyed my looking away.

After a while, the exhibit was like one big look-fest. Who cared about the art hanging on the walls? Most of us were more interested in the other people.

I wanted to get out my sketchbook and draw all the lines running between people's eyes, like laser beams. I saw these lines everywhere. The eye lines, the like lines, the I-want-to-know-you lines.

ℒ

Dad and I had lunch in the museum cafe.

Click, click, click. Dad was taking shots of me with his camera. "That exhibit made me itch to take some pictures of my own," he said.

Almost without thinking, I did my lazy model thing for Dad. Shifted around in my chair, got in different positions. I didn't like having my picture taken by other people. With Dad, I was so used to it, I hardly thought about it. He'd been taking pictures of me ever since I came to live with him when I was six.

I assumed he'd delete most of them anyway. Unless he wanted thirty pictures of his daughter eating a slice of the pepperoni and anchovy pizza we were sharing.

"I'm just one big photo-op for you, Dad," I said. I placed the back of one hand under my chin in a sophisticated model pose. *Click.*

"That's right, Amy-kins." *Click, click.* "I can't help it, though. You're so supercalifragilisticphotogenic."

I put the other hand on top of my head. Definitely not a

sophisticated model pose. "I sure wasn't in those pictures you took of me at Christmas with your family."

"They're your family, too, darling."

I bit my lower lip. I always got that wrong. I supposed Dad's family was my family, sort of. Somehow I never quite felt it, though. "Your" always came out instead of "my."

"You don't like the photos anyone takes of you at family gatherings," Dad said.

"That's because I stick out like a sore thumb."

Those photos always showed a bunch of white faces surrounding a caramel-colored one. Mine.

"I feel the same way at those events, honey," Dad said, patting my hand. "Someday we can write our memoirs together. We'll call it *The Two Sore Thumbs That Stuck Out.*"

Dad put his thumb next to mine on the table. The big white thumb with the smaller, darker one.

"How do *you* stick out?" I asked.

"As the only single person over twenty-five." Dad set down his camera and grabbed a slice of pizza. "At this point, every adult in our family is married down to the last second cousin. Except Bobbie, and he's been with his girlfriend so long, it's as if they're married."

"I like that about"—I caught myself—"our family."

"You're such a romantic, kiddo. You believe everyone should get together with someone, and they should go strolling through life two-by-two forever and ever."

"Yeah, I do." I stuck up my chin, to show I meant it.

Dad opened his mouth to say something. Then he seemed to decide he'd rather take a big bite of pizza.

Closing my eyes, I remembered my favorite picture in a book Aunt Meg, Dad's sister-in-law, had given me, *Bible Stories for the Young.* The animals walked up the gangplank into the Ark, each paired with another of the same type. Two tigers, two bears, two ostriches. They all had happy smiles on their faces because they were in couples. In the story, God said to Noah, "Bring your family and two of every kind of animal." It was only when I got older that I found out God meant a guy tiger and girl tiger. As a pro-gay kid who loved her gay dad, I decided to ignore that little detail.

Dad looked at his watch. "I know it'll happen any minute now."

"What?" I said.

"You'll start in about how I should find a boyfriend. Please, sweetie, I already get enough of that from your grandma. At Christmas she told me, 'Your dad and I would be so glad if you got married too.' She thinks she's being nice. Really, it's just pressure."

Dad sighed, rubbing his beard with one hand. "Now Mom and Dad's fortieth wedding anniversary is only six weeks away, and there will be even more talk about love and marriage going together like a horse and carriage, and it's all pressure, pressure, pressure."

I didn't understand the bit about the horse and carriage. I assumed it was a line from some song in a musical, because Dad loved musicals.

"Why don't you hurry up and get married in that case?" I was about to lick some tomato sauce off my fingers, then remembered Dad would scold me if I didn't use my napkin. "It's legal now."

Dad laughed. He had a boomy, big-guy laugh. "More pressure. I fought to get the right. Now I feel I'd better gosh-darn use it."

"At least date someone, Dad," I said. "You haven't gone on a date in months. And stop stealing my anchovies."

Dad pulled his hand back from the pizza slice I'd put down on my plate. "I thought you didn't like anchovies."

"I think maybe I'm changing my mind about that. But if you keep eating them all, I can't make any new taste tests."

5

"As for my going on a date," Dad said, "you know I've been crazy busy with work lately. I don't have time to go out with every Tom, Dick, and Harry on Match.com."

"Dad, in the fall when I told you I was too busy to try out for *The Wiz*, you said you were tired of people using being busy as an excuse. You said a person could always make the time if he wanted. You said—"

"Young lady, it isn't good manners to quote someone back to himself." Dad stood up. "Let's go see what's for dessert."

We walked over to the glass case where the three desserts were displayed. Three seconds later—which was one second of thought per dessert—I said, "I want the banana nut bread, the end piece." The end pieces were the best.

"The banana nut bread does look delicious," Dad said. "On the other hand, I love love love apple pie. And then there's the carrot cake."

Dad asked the man behind the counter which dessert he recommended. Next, he asked a woman standing near us which one she thought looked best. Having apple pie would bring back memories of childhood, Dad said. But banana nut bread was so strangely satisfying. On the other hand, the presence of a vegetable in carrot cake made it seem healthier.

Finally, Dad said, "Amy, which one should I have?"

I rolled my eyes. "Let's just go shares-ese with the banana nut bread. It's a big piece."

Back at our table, I said, "Dad, it took you five and a half hours to decide what to have for dessert. Correction: it took you that long *not* to decide. You always have so much trouble making choices."

Dad sighed. "I know. Imagine how hard it is for me to decide whether I should date Mr. Apple Pie or Mr. Carrot Cake. I'm starting to think the only way I'll ever find a boyfriend is if someone else selects the right person for me."

I stopped chewing my bite of banana nut bread.

I had a thought. Actually, three thoughts strung together.

Dad had trouble making choices.

Maybe he needed someone else to choose for him.

Maybe that someone was—well, me. After all, I cared about my dad and wanted him to be happy.

I swallowed the bite and said, "Why don't you date Dr. Van Patten?" Dr. Van Patten was my dentist.

Dad smiled. "There's just one teensy weensy problem with your idea."

"What's that?"

"Dr. Van Patten is already married to a very nice lady. Thanks for picking someone who makes good money, though."

I bit my knuckle. Biting my knuckle sometimes helped me think. "What about Hugh?"

"Precious, Hugh is my friend. You don't just add 'boy' to 'friend' to make someone a boyfriend."

Despite more knuckle biting, I'd already run out of ideas. That was annoying.

Leaving the rest of the banana nut bread to Dad, I got out my sketchbook and began drawing. A wall with some photos hanging on it. Some doodle-bug people with big pop-out eyes gawking at the photos, at each other.

After a while, I said, "Dad, if you want me to do my homework tonight, I think you should do yours."

"What homework?"

"About the boyfriend thing." I looked at Dad with my eyebrows pushed way up. I'd done this a few days ago in an argument with my best friend, Grace Kwan. I'd found it worked pretty well at the right moment.

Dad's big-guy laugh boomed out. "All right, all right! We'll have a study session together this evening."

I kept drawing in my sketchbook. Drawing lines like laser beams between one doodled figure and another. Eye lines, like lines, I-want-to-know-you lines.

Chapter 2

"Couldn't these turkeys at least run a spell-check on their profiles?" Dad exclaimed, sitting at his computer that evening.

"Uh-huh," I said.

Dad was doing his "homework" on Match.com. His computer sat on a table in the bay window of our living room. As a big guy, he didn't like desks because he was always banging his legs against some part of them. So instead he used a table.

I was curled up in my favorite spot, on the blue couch across from the fireplace, at the end closest to the window. I'd already done my own homework. All except for putrid Algebra. I'd left that for last.

"Another photo with sunglasses," Dad said, his gaze on the computer screen. "What are these guys thinking?"

"Really?" I didn't have enough brain power to work on Algebra *and* make smart comments. "Uh-huh" and "Really?" was about all I could manage.

Five minutes later, I snapped shut my Algebra textbook and yelled, "Finished!" I decided to reward myself by doing something fun. I took the big mirror off the wall, propped it against the couch, and plunked myself down on the floor cross-legged in front of it. I was going to draw my very first self-portrait. I was sure it would be amazing.

My eyes went up to the mirror, down to my sketchbook. Up, down, up, down. After ten minutes, my self-portrait was coming out like a cross between Natasha Obama and Mr. Potato Head. But closer to Mr. P.

My cat Flora lay on her own favorite spot at the other end of the couch. Flora had gorgeous ginger fur, white paws, and eyes the color of jade. Right now, her white paws were curled under her and her jade-colored eyes partly open, watching me.

Flora and I communicated telepathically. At least, I sent her messages in my mind and was pretty sure she responded. Dissatisfied with my drawing, I telepathed to her, *How did Rembrandt and those other old geniuses make doing a self-portrait seem so easy?*

Flora stared at me with her round green eyes and telepathed back, *Perhaps your drawing skills aren't the problem, dear. Perhaps it's the way you look.*

Was that true? I studied myself some more in the mirror. A squinting Amy McDougall studied back.

Dad was always telling me I was pretty. He kept saying that until it got annoying, like anything a parent told you about yourself, even if it was nice. But my looks were so…in between.

My mom was from Guatemala, and my birth father was African American. That was almost the only thing I knew about him, aside from the fact that my mom had met him in rehab. Great place to go boyfriend shopping, Mom.

My African American genes were stronger in my skin, which was more black than brown. My Guatemalan genes kicked in with my hair, which was more straight than kinky. I was an "interesting mix," as Dad said.

I drew a smaller face behind Natasha Potato Head, over her right shoulder. A woman's face, not very clear. I gave her my hair—was that right? Gave her a similar nose, similar eyes, without being sure about those things either.

What did my mom look like? It had been so long since I'd seen her.

I lived with my mom until I was four. That ended with me wandering around the streets with a note pinned to my jacket saying, "My name is Amy."

My mom had left me with a woman friend. She told the friend she'd come get me the next day. Two days passed, and my mom never came, because she was doing drugs or got arrested for shoplifting or who knew what. The friend got tired of having me in her place. Her bright idea was to put me out on the street.

In the end, the police found me. They asked, "Where's your mommy?" I said, "I don't know."

The authorities took me away from my mom. I spent the next couple of years bouncing from one foster home to another. I saw my mom one afternoon a week at the Department of Social Services.

Junk food, games, and daylight—that was what I remembered about those visits. Mom would bring me junk food, and play games with me, and it was always daylight outside....

Dad's voice snapped me back to the present.

"Amy-pie, this guy has a picture of himself at a funeral. Doesn't that seem odd?"

"Maybe he looks good in black," I said. Dad kept finding reasons to nix guys. I didn't want to encourage him.

"Should I go on a date with someone named Zero?"

I stood up, trying to get a better view of the screen. "What does he look like?"

Dad shooed me away. "Never mind, darling. This is something Daddy has to figure out for himself."

I dropped back onto the rug and grabbed my sketchbook. I drew a face over my left shoulder. Dad's. This face I knew very well. It was big and square-ish, with short light brown hair. I scribbled in Dad's beard. I considered getting my colored pencils from my bedroom to show how his beard had more red in it than the hair on his head. I was too lazy, though, and stuck to black and white.

When I was six, I went to a Christmas party at an adoption agency. One of the workers from the agency introduced me to Dad. Dad talked to me about the gingerbread man cookie I was eating. He said, "I'm like you. I eat the legs first, then the arms. It just seems wrong to start with the head."

I didn't realize at first that the agency had set up our meeting, that this guy was looking for someone to adopt. After that, Dad and I went on some outings together, to the park, the zoo. Then I did get the picture. We were supposed to see if we wanted to become father and daughter. Sort of like trying on a pair of shoes to make sure they fit.

Before I went home with Dad, my social worker asked if I was okay with having a father who was gay. I sort of knew what that meant, and I said yes. Dad liked guys, I got that. I guessed I liked guys, too. Still, I didn't see why that meant he couldn't also marry some nice lady. Edith, Grace's mom, for example. Edith was divorced, and Dad got along really well with her. That way, Grace and I could be sisters.

When I was nine, I asked Dad, "Why don't you marry Edith?"

He gave me that Dad Look that said, Someday you'll understand, kid.

When I got older, I did understand. Dad liked guys, and he wasn't going to marry a woman. Period.

Dad was still looking at dating profiles and talking to the screen.

"Great shot of the Golden Gate Bridge," he said. "Not so great of you."

A few minutes later, Dad stood up and stretched his arms over his head. "That's enough mug shots for one night. Princess and the Pea, you can have fifteen minutes on my computer while I clean the kitchen, then off to bed."

I wasn't so pathetic that I didn't have my own computer. But my computer *was* pathetic. It was Dad's old one and did everything r e a l l y s l o w l y. So Dad let me use his zippy new computer when he wasn't.

"How many guys did you write to, Dad?" I asked.

He was already heading down the hall toward the kitchen. "I was very selective," he called back over his shoulder.

Sitting down at Dad's computer, I clicked on New Tab. I went onto my Facebook page. "You have two pokes, eighteen messages." I didn't care about the pokes. Pokes were lame. As for the eighteen messages, I knew they were all group ones from Grace and Miranda about some dumb Journalism Club thing. Bored, I let my eyes slide over one tab to Match, which Dad had left open.

I was curious to know more about what Dad was up to with his guy search. I clicked on Match, then on My Profile. I read, "I already have one great 'long-term relationship,' the one with my thirteen-year-old daughter." Thanks, Dad.

Dad's profile shot showed him lying on his side on a lawn, leaning on one elbow. I'd snapped that photo myself in Golden Gate Park. There was my very own shadow on Dad's chest and his right shoulder. He'd scolded me for getting it in the picture. "That's the sign of an amateur," he'd told me.

I glanced over at Flora and telepathed, *I guess he liked this picture taken by an amateur, because he's using it in his profile.*

Don't talk to me about dating, Flora telepathed back. *I have no interest in the subject. I'm self-sufficient, and I believe everyone else should be that way too.*

I clicked on Mailbox, then Sent. Dad hadn't sent any messages that evening. Not a single freaking one. That was what he meant by being "very selective."

When I went to My Last Search, photos of about thirty guys popped up. I clicked on the first one. Why hadn't Dad sent a love letter flying off to him? He seemed all right. He had a nice smile.

Bap, bap, bap went the wooden spoon in the kitchen down the hall. I knew Dad was knocking it against a pot to get off the last of the brown rice.

If I'd been a cartoon character, an idea light bulb would have appeared above my head at that moment. The idea made my heart beat faster and my palms sweat. What had Dad said in the cafe that afternoon? *Maybe I need someone else to choose the right person for me.*

I clicked on Email Him. I started to write an email to the guy with the nice smile. But what was I supposed to say?

"Five minutes!" Dad called from the kitchen. Then he yelled-sang a song from one of his musicals about how "the rain in Spain stayed mainly on the plain." As for me, I muttered-sang,

Your singing is a pain
And I wish you would refrain
So my goal I can attain.

In the upper left corner of Nice Smile's profile, I spotted a box called Icebreaker. Break the ice. That sounded right. I clicked on it. And that was all I had to do. Bingo! Match sent off an Icebreaker, the way they did in the Arctic when a ship got stuck in the ice.

I skimmed through the other profiles in My Last Search. With each profile, it took me one to ten seconds to decide thumbs-up or down. Two seconds to send an Icebreaker racing through internet space to the thumbs-up guy. Then I moved on to the next.

I'd gotten about halfway through the profiles when I heard Dad coming down the hall. I clicked over one tab.

Putting his hands on my shoulders, Dad looked at the screen. "Anything new on Facade Book?" he asked.

"Nope," I said. "Same old same old." I was glad that standing behind me, Dad didn't have a good view of my face. The guilty expression on it would have made him suspect I was up to something.

"Good night, Princess Leah," Dad said to me as I headed for my room. "Sweet dreams."

At first, lying in bed, I didn't have sweet dreams or any other kind. Instead, I stared at the ceiling and twirled a lock of my hair round and round. This was a bad habit I had, twirling my hair when I was anxious. My second-grade teacher got so tired of my doing it, she fastened down the part of my hair I kept twirling with a piece of adhesive tape. I must have been anxious a lot in second grade.

"What have I done?" I said to myself. I didn't know anything about those Icebreaker guys. That one with the humongous tattoo on his arm looked kind of mean. What if he was an ax murderer and ax-murdered my dad?

I spun my lock of hair faster and faster and faster.

The next evening, Dad was at his computer reading the *New York Times*. I sat on the couch with my laptop, trying to make a crossword puzzle for my school paper, the *Maroon Baboon*.

"This on-line program is cool," I told Dad. "You type in words and clues, and the program turns them into a crossword puzzle."

Dad was squinting at his screen. "Scientists have found these frogs in Ecuador that actually change the texture of their skin."

Flora sat beside me with her tail wrapped around her. I telepathed, *Why is Dad reading about frogs in Ecuador when he should be checking his messages on Match?*

Flora didn't respond. She was probably meditating. She meditated a lot.

I did what I could to influence Dad. "The program *matches* up the different words."

"The frogs don't change just their color, but their actual skin texture."

"I'm trying to theme the puzzle around *romance*."

"Scientists assume the frogs do this to camouflage themselves from predators."

"I use words like *boyfriend* and *date* and *crush*."

"Sounds good." That was what Dad said to me when he wasn't really listening.

While I was pretty sure cats couldn't actually roll their eyes, sometimes I thought I almost caught Flora doing it—like just then. She telepathed to me, *Nice try with the subliminal suggestions, dear. I recommend a good loud meow. That usually gets me what I want.*

Finally I said, "Dad, will you be through with your computer soon? This program is running so slowly on mine."

"Sure, cupcake," Dad said. "Just let me do a few more things."

From where I sat, I could see Dad's screen well enough to recognize Match when it came up. I made a face at Flora. Even without telepathy, it communicated, *Shows how much you know, kitty cat.*

"What the—?" Dad exclaimed. "Six messages?...'Thank you for your interest.' What interest? He must be crazy. Delete.... Hmm, this guy looks kind of scary, with that big tattoo on his arm. Delete.... That's weird. These are all guys who came up in my search last night."

While Dad deleted all his messages, I tried to look like I was concentrating hard on my puzzle. I wanted to ask, "What's a word that means 'idea that was a total bust and you sure hope your dad never finds out about'?"

CHAPTER 3

If someone had made a movie about my life, the list of filming locations would have been short.

One: my home.

Two: my school.

Three: Grace's home.

Four: my therapist's office, where I spent fifty minutes every week reassuring my therapist I wasn't screwed up, even though I'd been adopted.

Five: the Department of Social Services, where I spent a half-hour every other week reassuring my social worker that my adoptive dad wasn't starving, abusing, or neglecting me.

Yes, tragically, the second most important location in my life after home was Everett Middle School, seven blocks from where I lived.

Dad said Everett was a beautiful old building. The entrance had five big columns and bright tiles around the doors.

Dad could say what he wanted about the outside—no way was the inside beautiful. The halls were painted three shades of yellow. Dark egg yolk on the floors, soft daisy petal on the walls, blinding day-glo for the lockers. The administration seemed to think that if it painted enough things yellow, we students would feel our school years were one long sunny day.

Guess again. Everett was like a maze in a lab experiment with too many rats running around in it. The classrooms were crowded, the hallways were crowded. At least the rats' maze wasn't so ratty and mazey when I navigated it with a friend. Luckily Grace and I had English together right before lunch.

Grace and I had been friends since second grade. We started out more like enemies. One day during recess, I grabbed her plaid cap when she left it on a bench because I liked it and wanted it. Grace chased after me. I shoved her and she fell down and cried. Helping Grace get up, one of the teachers scolded, "Amy McDougall, you should be ashamed of yourself!"

When I had time to think things over, I *was* ashamed. So a month later I invited Grace to my birthday party. And because I'd invited her to mine, she invited me to hers. Soon I discovered I liked other things about Grace besides that cap.

Grace's parents came from Hong Kong. She was short and took fast steps to keep up with me when we walked, because I was almost a head taller. She was terrible at sports. Sometimes I couldn't help making a joke about her being called Grace and not having any.

Grace's body might not have been talented, but her mind was. She got straight As, even an A-minus in Gym, because at least she tried really hard.

After the Icebreaker fiasco, I decided I'd better get some advice from Straight A Grace. As we headed out of English and down the ramp to the first floor, I told her I was trying to find my dad a boyfriend.

Grace adjusted her glasses, pushing them all of half a millimeter up her nose. "Exactly how do you intend to do that?"

"I have no idea. That's where you come in. You need to think up a plan."

We'd reached the bottom of the ramp. I was about to head for the courtyard when Grace grabbed my arm.

"We have to go to the cafeteria so I can buy something," she said, pulling me in that direction.

"Didn't your mom make you one of her amazing lunches?" I asked.

Edith made the best lunches. Nothing so boring as a mere sandwich. Instead, several plastic containers each with some incredibly delicious type of Chinese food. That was one reason I used to want her for my new mom.

"She's super busy at work and didn't have time," Grace said. "Come on, it'll only take a minute."

Grace knew I hated the cafeteria. Unless it was raining, I didn't care how cold it was outside, I was sitting in the courtyard, not in the cafeteria. The sky was clear today except for a few cotton ball clouds, so I'd hoped to have a cafeteria-free lunch hour.

As I let Grace drag me along, I moaned, "Gracie, the things I do for you!"

The cafeteria was as bad as ever. Filled with young rats buying food, chowing down on food, spilling food, tossing food in the trash. The only food-related thing they weren't doing was throwing it at each other. Not yet.

Grace grabbed one of the blue trays, and we got in line. We were stuck between a guy behind us who was in a hurry and kept poking me with his tray, and a girl ahead who wasn't and kept gabbing with a friend instead of moving forward.

Grace stood on her toes and squinted to see the menu up ahead. "What should I have? The veggie stir fry? Or maybe cheesy potato soup and a salad?"

"I bet you won't like the stir fry. It won't be as good as your mom's."

Grace peered at a bowl of fruit on one of the glass shelves. "Yech, these bananas don't even look ripe." She grabbed an orange instead. "Now about your dad—why can't he find a boyfriend himself?"

"My dad is good at a lot of things," I said. "Some things he's lousy at, though. Like he can't ice-skate or roller-blade or do anything else where you need a sense of balance. I think boyfriend finding is another thing he's lousy at. I mean, he hasn't had a boyfriend in almost a year."

"You're thinking in teen years," Grace said. "A year for an adult isn't so long. It's like human years versus dog years."

Finally we made it to the courtyard, which was almost as crowded and noisy as the cafeteria. All those kids who hadn't had a thing to say when teachers asked us questions in class had a lot to say now. Say or shout.

In the center of the courtyard was a flagpole without a flag. Four stone benches surrounded it, facing away. A couple of girls were just leaving one bench, and Grace and I slipped into their place.

"Anyway, I need your advice about how to find him the right person," I said.

Grace ate a mouthful of veggies. "What's in it for me, Amy Baby?"

Dad had nicknames for me, and so did Grace. One was Amy Baby, because I was all of one month younger than she was.

"A huge scoop of gratitude," I said.

"And?"

"That glow of satisfaction you get when you help a friend."

Grace craned her neck toward my lunch bag. "Can you bribe me with something good to eat? This stir fry is terrible."

"I told you not to get it." I jiggled a plastic bag. "Scrumptious carrot sticks."

Grace made a face. "What have you got for dessert?"

I held up another bag. It contained brown carob cubes flecked with sunflower seeds. "Yummy energy nuggets."

Grace made an even worse face. "I should have known. Nothing but your usual health food crap. Fat free, sugar free, taste free."

"These nuggets are actually pretty good. Come on, I'll give you two."

Grace wrinkled her nose in a way that meant, You'd better improve your offer or I'll probably say no.

"Three," I said.

"Oh, all right." Grace held out her hand. She bit into an energy nugget. And she put on her Grace Thinking Hard expression.

After a minute, she asked, "Can you find your dad a boyfriend where he works?"

"Not very likely. Dad runs his own business, and he's alone in his studio most of the time."

"Can he meet someone he's taking pictures of?"

"He almost never takes pictures of people for work. Usually it's stuff for sale on websites. Laptops and bikes and things like that."

"Yeah," Grace said, "and most bikes aren't ready for a long-term relationship. They just want to keep moving on. How about a neighbor? I forget who else lives in your building."

"Old Mrs. Reynolds lives below us. Above us, a gay guy—but he already has a partner."

"How inconsiderate!"

Ten minutes of "What about?—no, never mind" and "There's always—but that wouldn't work" didn't get us anywhere.

"You get a big fat F in Boyfriend Finding," I said.

Grace threw up her hands. "There goes my GPA!"

"My dad needs a boyfriend to take to his parents' wedding anniversary so he won't feel like a pathetic single. That's only a month and a half away. The clock is ticking, Grace."

She patted my arm. "Don't worry. I've planted the problem in my brain like a seed. I'm sure some amazing scheme will sprout at any moment."

"That's the worst simile I've ever heard in my entire life." Ms. Galland had been teaching us about similes in English.

"If I were you, I wouldn't be so critical of a friend when you want that friend's help."

"Sorry! Pretty please keep coming up with ideas."

"My latest idea is that your dad will be ticked off if you drag home some guy and say, 'Hey, Dad, I've found you the perfect boyfriend.' That's called butting into someone else's business. Parents are fine with butting into *our* business, but they freak out if we do it to them."

Instead of throwing away my empty plastic bags, I put them in my backpack so Dad could use them again tomorrow. Dad was Mr. Re-use and Recycle.

"How dumb do you think I am?" I said. "I won't let Dad know I'm cooking up a romance for him. He's got to believe it's something he cooked up himself. Or"—I tried to think of the right word— "or fate did."

"I see. Love is like a flowerpot that gets knocked off a window sill and falls on your head while you're walking down the street."

I slipped Grace's glasses off her face, put them on, and looked at her over the top of the rims, the way Ms. Galland looked over hers. "Ms. Galland said similes should be *concise*."

"Okay. Love is like a flowerpot."

Chapter 4

Later in our talk, Grace did give me one good piece of advice. Before I set off on the great boyfriend hunt, I should learn more about what kind of guy Dad wanted. I tried to sound him out while we were making dinner that evening.

"Dad," I said, "what do you think the ideal boyfriend is like?"

"For me, or you, or folks in general?" Dad asked. He didn't look up from a recipe for Tuna Curry in a Hurry.

"Let's start with you," I said.

"Well…" Dad began.

I listened carefully, then put what he said in an email that I sent to Grace.

Travis McDougall's Recipe for the Perfect Boyfriend

1 cup charm
1 and ½ cups kindness
1 can intelligence
1 package sense of humor
1 tablespoon spirituality
2 teaspoons wickedness
1 pinch common sense
Salt and pepper hair to taste

Bake for approximately thirty-five years, depending on oven

Comments: When making for teenage girls, reduce baking time and leave out the wickedness.

Grace wrote back, "OMG, I made this dish myself, and it was soooooo yummo."

I wrote, "But does Dad's recipe help me at all?"

Grace sent back an image of a doughnut. That was our symbol for "Dunno."

❧

Later that evening, Dad let me use his computer again. I noticed he'd left Match open. I decided to take another shot at it. I'd be picky this time and just write to one guy.

This was San Francisco, so there were a jillion guy-seeking-guy profiles. I typed "kids" in Match's Search. As in "wants kids." That got me a quarter of a jillion. I started clicking and reading. I felt like I was pushing my cart down an aisle in a supermarket.

"I'm mellow and shy."

Maybe.

"I'm smart and have a sense of humor."

Maybe to you, too.

"I love to cycle, swim, and hike."

Dad liked doing those things.

"I'm into movies, theater, country outings."

Ditto.

"I believe in karma and live by it."

Pass.

"1966 model, low mileage, high performance."

Huh? Pass.

Then I found the profile for Clearbluewater.

> All we need is a sunny room
> Where time moves slow
> And love can grow.
> All we need is a double bed
> To keep us close when things are said.
> And on stormy nights,
> I'll hold you tight.
> The rest, my dear,

We'll play by ear,
In our sunny room.

My mind jammed for four seconds picturing Dad and Clearbluewater tangled up in that double bed. I wanted Dad to have a boyfriend, but I didn't want the whole thing to be so—well, in my face.

On the fifth second, I took a deep breath and my mind unjammed. After all, Clearbluewater sounded like he might have at least some of the ingredients in Dad's recipe.

I thought for a minute, chewing on my lower lip. Then I typed.

> *Dear Clearbluewater,*
> *I like your profile. I hope you like mine. If you write back, please pretend you're making the first move. This is just my thing. It's the only weird thing about me.*
> *Yours truly,*
> *Phototype*

DELETE

> *Dear Clearbluewater,*
> *I'm a friend of Phototype. He's shy, so I thought I would—*

DELETE

Okay, I said to myself. I'll just tell the truth.

> *Dear Clearbluewater,*
> *I'm writing for my dad. He's a great guy. I think you two might hit it off. He's kind of shy, though, and he needs help meeting people. Please write to him if you're interested, but don't say I contacted you.*
> *Amy*

I just had time to finish this message before I heard Dad coming down the hall. I clicked Send.

Chapter 5

Amy is so smart, Amy is so smart, Amy is so smart. Write that on a piece of paper fifty-five times!

A few days later, Dad told me he was going on a date. "You say I never date, but I'm going on a date this evening."

"Who with?" I asked.

"This guy who wrote me on Match. His name is Bart. Bart did his profile as a poem. Wasn't that creative?"

Jackpot!

An hour later, the doorbell rang.

"We're walking up the street to Duboce Park," Dad told me, putting on his jacket. "We want to watch the dogs."

"Great," I said. "Take your time."

Since I was the one who'd found this guy for Dad, of course I wanted to sneak a peek at him. That wasn't easy, because when the bell rang, instead of letting Bart come up to the apartment, Dad went downstairs to meet him at the street door. I raced across the living room and glued myself to the left side of the bay window. Not literally.

I had a clear view of Dad and Bart for all of two seconds before they walked under a sycamore. It was spring, and the stupid tree was covered with big stupid green leaves. I could hardly see Bart and Dad at all through them. I found out Bart had brown hair. That was about all.

Naturally I wanted to spy on those two. It was like I'd carved DAD + BART on a tree trunk. I was eager to find out if I should carve a heart around their names too.

I ran to my closet and pulled out a beige trench coat. I was sorry I'd bought this coat five minutes after I left the thrift store where I found it. As if I could wear a trench coat to school without the other kids sniggering. Still, it was perfect for spying. Dad had never seen the coat because I'd never ever worn it.

I grabbed a wig from the Halloween costume box in Dad's closet. Then, worried Dad might recognize the wig, I threw a scarf over my head. Finally, just in case the rest of my disguise wasn't enough, I slapped on dark glasses I'd found on the street.

Duboce Park was a big lawn with some trees around the edge. Dad called it "Dog-oce Park." It seemed like it was more a place for dogs to enjoy themselves than for people. Though there were some people, too, because the dogs brought their owners.

Hurrying along Duboce Street, I spotted Dad and Bart as they entered the park. They sat down on a bench at the other end. They watched the dogs, like Dad said they would. I sat on a bench far away from them. There was no way Dad could tell who I was because I almost couldn't tell who he was, and he wasn't in disguise.

Dad and Bart watched the dogs and talked. And talked and watched. And watched and talked and pointed at the dogs.

After a half-hour, I came to the conclusion it was boring being a spy. The sun had set by now, and the wind was picking up. Even in my trench coat and wig and scarf, I was getting cold. I thought how nice it would be to have a big steaming mug of hot chocolate. At last I headed home.

In case Dad brought Bart back with him and wanted some privacy, I stayed in my room while I drank my chocolate. I loved my room, so I didn't mind spending time there. Dad said that when he showed it to me for the first time, my eyes got big and I asked, "You mean I have this room all to myself?" With my foster-care parents, I'd always had to share with other kids.

I slipped on my fuzzy pink slippers and plugged in the string of little white lights that wound around my headboard. Sitting down at my desk, I powered on my crappy old laptop. While it was taking forever to start, I chose a candle from my collection to light. Tonight I was in the mood for Ginger Dusk.

After a few sips of chocolate, my computer was finally ready. I put on my headphones and clicked on the latest Justin Bieber video.

Sliding my slipper off and on my right foot, I wondered how Dad and Bart were getting along. I drew a picture of them in my sketchbook. They sat on a bench in the park, a circle of dog faces surrounding them. Not knowing what Bart looked like aside from the brown hair, I made him into Leonardo DiCaprio. Leonardo was one of Dad's movie star crushes.

I worked hard on that drawing. Used my colored pencils to create the trees and lawn and bench. Gave each dog a different face. Dad and Bart I did with my trusty Number 2 pencil, kept very sharp. With a lot of erasing and re-doing, I managed to get Dad to look like Dad and Bart to look like Leonardo. I drew lines that ran from Dad's eyes to Bart's, flashing laser beams binding them together.

The better and more detailed I made the drawing, the more it felt like magic. The white kind, of course. If I drew it, and drew it well, wouldn't that help make it happen?

Later, I heard the street door close, then Dad coming up the stairs. I could tell he was taking the steps two at a time. That was always a sign he was in a good mood.

He stuck his head into my room. "You okay, sweet pea?"

"I'm fine," I said. "How were the dogs?"

"The dogs? Oh, fine."

It was almost ten, but Dad didn't say, "Time for bed, young lady." He didn't ask if I'd done my homework. His mind must have been elsewhere. Somewhere nice, since he had a big smile on his face.

❧

A few days later, I was at home, coming down the hall. I heard Dad on his phone in the living room.

"Hi, it's Travis. I'm breaking the rule.... The rule about not calling someone for at least a week after the first date."

Bart.

"The rules are right there on the official How to Date website. You just haven't looked." Dad chuckled, though he sounded nervous too.

"So listen, I was wondering if you wanted to get together.... No, you're kidding.... Really? Well, I guess I should say congratulations. So—congratulations.... Of course, of course, okay, okay, yeah, bye."

I counted to ten, then went into the living room.

Dad looked over at me. "Remember that guy Bart I went on a date with?"

I scrunched up my face like I was trying hard to remember. "Oh yeah!"

"Yesterday, his ex told him he wanted them to get back together," Dad said. "And they did."

And that was the last I heard of Bart the Poet of Match.com. I tore that picture out of my sketchbook and threw it away.

Amy is not so smart, Amy is not so smart, Amy is not so smart. I'd better write *that* on a piece of paper fifty-five times.

Chapter 6

Sometimes good things practically fell into my lap. Like the sateen baseball jacket I bought for only three bucks at a garage sale. It fit me perfectly. I got lots of compliments the first time I wore it to school.

A good thing practically fell into my lap while I was boyfriend hunting for Dad. Or seemed to.

A week after the Bart business, Grace and I were sitting at her kitchen table playing Monopoly. Edith was making brownies and talking on and on. Edith talked a lot. Her English was good, though she still had a Chinese accent. Edith was a landscape designer. Today she was talking about how much one of her clients kept—talking.

"Vera was telling me all about her family," Edith said. "I wanted to say, 'Lady, time is money. You're telling me the cute things your granddaughter did when we should be deciding whether to plant rosemary or lavender beside your new brick steps.'"

Grace and I let just enough of Edith's talk filter through for us to make a response once in a while. Like, "Oh really?"

Then Edith was talking about another landscape designer in her firm, Kevin. She said Kevin made extra money "flipping houses." When she said this, Grace and I flipped over a couple of our green Monopoly houses. We laughed.

"Kevin will buy a house and fix it up real cute. He's an artistic type; he went to the Art Institute here in the city. Then the real estate market took a dip, and he was stuck with this house way out in the Contra Costa boonies that he couldn't sell. He ended up living in it. Poor Kevin, he says he's surrounded by all these rednecks. That's especially hard for a gay person—"

I stopped, just about to roll the dice. Grace and I looked at each other. Gay guy, artistic type, went to the Art Institute, where my dad had studied.

I pointed at Grace. Discreetly, so her mom wouldn't notice. She pointed back at me. I pointed harder at her, mouthing, "No, you." Finally I won, though she did make one of our gestures: pointed at me, made a circle in the air, then pointed at herself. For "you owe me."

"How old is Kevin, Mom?" Grace asked in her most innocent voice.

Edith poured the gooey brown batter into a pan. "Mid-thirties."

"And you like him?"

"Oh yeah, Kevin is a great guy. He talks fast, and a lot." Someone else talking a lot. Must be a trend. "But at least what he says is usually interesting."

"Mom, I feel sorry for Kevin, living out in the boonies that way. Why don't we invite him to dinner?" Then as if it had just occurred to her, "Hey, we could invite Travis, too. They might enjoy each other."

Edith popped the brownies in the oven. "That's a good idea, Grace. I was about to ask Amy and Travis over on their own, but really it's as easy to cook for five people as for four. You still have to buy the same ingredients and..."

Grace and I went back to tuning Edith out. We probably wouldn't tune her in again until the brownies were done and she asked if we wanted some.

It took about six months for Grace and me to become best friends after our tussle in the school yard over her cap. Because we were best friends, Grace and I were always going to each other's home, with Dad picking me up, or Edith picking up Grace. After a while, the four of us started doing things together. We'd rent a rowboat on Stow Lake, or go to the zoo, or have lunch in Chinatown, where Edith knew the best places to eat.

After a while, Dad and Edith became best friends too. They never exactly said they were, because adults just didn't do that. But when they were yacking away together, Grace and I would look at them, and one of us would whisper, "BFF," and the other would nod.

Sometimes Dad would have Edith and Grace over for dinner. More often, Edith would have us over. Dad was a good cook, but Edith was a fantastic one.

That Saturday, Edith made a dinner for the four of us plus her friend Kevin. It included a couple of my favorite dishes of hers, smashed cucumbers with ginger, and cabbage salad with roasted peanuts.

Kevin had one of those beards without a mustache, like Abe Lincoln. Edith was right, he did talk a lot. He and Edith were neck and neck in the Talking-A-Lot competition.

"I'm from L.A.," Kevin babbled on, "but a friend says I should tell people I'm from New York, which would explain so much about me, why I talk and walk and think so fast."

Kevin talked about flipping houses, and the paintings he made, and his landscape projects. He said he wanted to have kids, a good sign. Four kids, to be exact. "I've already chosen names for them," he told us.

"If you're adopting," Dad pointed out, "they'll probably already have their own names. Like this young lady here." He nodded at me, smiling.

"I did get Dad's last name," I said, "after the adoption was official."

"That just made things simpler at school and when we traveled," Dad said.

Kevin said, "Tell me how you two ended up together. I'd be interested to know. Maybe I'll have to be a single dad, too. It's so hard to find the right partner to have kids with."

"I filled out a million forms," Dad said, "and answered a million questions. After that, I went to an adoption agency and looked through a binder with photos of kids and reports about them—"

Kevin barged in. "And you spotted a photo of Amy, and bells rang and lights flashed, and you said to yourself, 'She's the one.' Is that what happened?"

"No," Dad said. "What happened is that it got harder and harder for me to turn the pages in the binder. I'd look at a photo of a kid and think, 'If I turn the page, that means I won't be adopting *you*.' When I explained this to the woman at the agency, she said she knew a kid she thought I should meet. 'I'm not sure why exactly,' she said, 'but I think you two might be right for each other.'"

"How sweet. It was like she played matchmaker for you. I wouldn't be surprised if she asked your astrological sign and your favorite color."

It was true, I thought. Someone had made a match for Dad and me all those years ago, a father and daughter one. And here I was trying to make another match for Dad, a boyfriend one.

Kevin gave a few quick tugs to his Abe Lincoln beard. "Go on, I'm dying to know what comes next. This is better than a movie."

Dad gestured to me. "Maybe Amy would like to help tell the story."

"Okay," I said. That should be easy, since I'd heard Dad tell it so often. Though buried in there somewhere, I was sure I did actually remember parts of it myself. "The woman arranged for Dad and me to meet at the agency's Christmas party."

Dad laughed. "I was so nervous on my way there. It was like going on a first date. This pipsqueak might tell me to get lost."

"At the party, Dad and I talked about things like the right way to eat a gingerbread cookie."

"She offered to show me her drawings. You know how most kids have just a jumble of artwork. Amy showed me this shoebox she'd decorated and used for storing hers. Her drawings were on pages she'd cut to fit in the shoebox. Creative, yet orderly."

I drank water from my glass to hide how big my smile was. I was proud of my Art Shoebox. I still had it in my closet.

Kevin almost jumped out of his chair. "Ah ha, and that's when it happened, the moment you saw that shoebox, you just knew she was the right kid for you, and bells rang, and—"

Dad held up his hand to stop him. "Wrong," he said. "You know how most kids draw pictures of houses, the outsides? Amy showed me a bunch of drawings of the insides of houses, with cozy couches and pictures on the walls. They made me think, This kid wants to come *inside* someone's home. Maybe *my* home. And wouldn't it be great to have her there, with her funny face and her cute giggle?"

Dad put his hand on Kevin's arm. "And *that*, Kevin," he said, "*that* is when it did happen. The bells rang, the lights flashed, and I knew this was the right kid for me."

Kevin applauded as if he were in a theater. "That's just the most adorable story. It's like you two were meant for each other. I'll have to look into the adopting thing, though not until I move out of the Wild Wild East of Contra Costa."

The dinner part of the evening was like a roller coaster ride where your car goes up and up, and your view gets better and better. Dad and Kevin seemed to have a lot to say to each other, and for once Edith hardly said anything. I liked to think she wanted to help me with my matchmaking.

Things changed when Edith served her strawberry shortcake—Edith liked to cook Chinese for dinner, American for dessert. Not that there was anything wrong with the shortcake. In fact, the problem was that it was a little too good.

Kevin: "Oh my God, this is the best dessert I've had in the last five years. No, the last ten years, and yes, Edith, I will let you talk me into having another piece, though not too big, well, but not that small either."

Kevin shouldn't have had that second piece, because afterward he babbled even more and even faster. "Oh my God, I'm having a sugar rush, this always happens when I eat too many sweets."

Then Kevin said he was going to pop out on the back porch to have a cigarette. Grace and I looked at each other. We knew my dad didn't like being around smokers. One big demerit for Kevin.

Later, Dad and Kevin got into an argument about Madonna versus Marilyn Monroe. "I only want to make one point," Dad said once, twice, three times, holding up a finger. Kevin just kept babbling over him.

While Kevin was defending Madonna—or Marilyn Monroe, afterward I couldn't remember which—he made this big gesture and knocked over his wine glass. The bad details: the glass had a lot of wine in it, and the wine was red, and most of it fell on Dad's shirt, which wasn't red.

Down, down, down plunged the roller coaster car, with the passengers screaming and feeling sick to their stomachs.

Sometimes it was bad things that practically fell into my lap. The second time I wore that fantastic sateen baseball jacket, I was standing under a tree when something heavy and wet splatted onto my shoulder. A slimy, partly green glob of pigeon poop.

❧

After the flop with Kevin, Grace thought I'd done enough to find Dad a boyfriend.

"Give something a chance to happen on its own," she said. "It's spring, after all. Maybe spring fever will drive your dad into some guy's arms."

I chewed one of my knuckles. "I've only set up Dad with two guys so far. I need to keep at it."

Grace gave me one of her long, hard looks. "Are you sure you aren't just being a bossy-pants? It's like you telling everyone in the Journalism Club what to do all the time."

"But—"

"Or like in seventh grade when you directed the school play, and you thought that meant telling us exactly how to speak every single line."

I opened my mouth to say something, then closed it. When a friend accused you of being a bossy-pants, it was hard to tell her to shut up.

Chapter 7

Besides Grace, the only person I told about my plan to matchmake for Dad was my therapist, Dr. Sophia Evans.

Ever since the Department of Social Services took me away from my mom, they said I had to see one of its social workers regularly, and I kind of had to see a therapist DSS paid for. My visits to my social worker and my therapist were part of my routine, like soccer or band practice for other kids.

A year ago, my therapist moved away. I asked Dad if I had to see another one.

"At your age, the Department of Social Services probably wouldn't insist," he said. "But I still think it's a good idea."

"Don't only nutcases need a therapist?" I asked.

"Of course not," Dad said.

I agreed to try out a new therapist. My last one was an older woman who wore round glasses that made her look like an owl. So I was surprised by Dr. Sophia Evans when she came to get me in the waiting room. She wasn't much taller than I was and only in her twenties. She had big brown eyes, curly hair the color of honey, and a thin silver ring through her left eyebrow.

My first question was, "How do I know you won't run to my dad and tell him everything I say?"

"That would be against my code of ethics as a therapist," Sophia said.

I was impressed. Not even Grace had a code of ethics that would keep her from blabbing all my secrets.

Sophia added, "Unless you say you're going to do something illegal, or that will harm yourself or another person."

Since I didn't intend to rob a bank or kill myself or anyone else, that seemed okay.

From then on, for fifty minutes every Wednesday afternoon, Sophia and I sat across from each other in matching green armchairs and talked. I felt I could say just about anything to her. Except that I wished she'd get rid of that stupid eyebrow ring. I kept staring at it and wondering what it felt like and whether her eyebrow hurt if she lay on it.

Sophia said things too. She wasn't like those therapists in movies who only said, "Uh-huh" and "Um-hum." One thing she told me about herself was that she'd been adopted, like me. She was the only other person I knew who'd been adopted.

At first, I didn't tell Sophia about my brilliant plan to matchmake for Dad. I'd found there was a problem with telling people about a brilliant plan: that they might say that actually it wasn't so brilliant and here was why. Adults were especially bad that way. Still, Sophia was sworn to secrecy, and I thought she might have some useful tips.

Soon after the Kevin dinner, I was talking with Sophia about what present I could get Dad for his birthday, which was a few weeks away. This seemed like a good time to bring up my plan.

"Maybe I should get Dad a new boyfriend," I said.

Sophia laughed. "That's a good idea. A boyfriend in a box with a ribbon around it."

"I'm serious."

"How do you know your dad wants a boyfriend?" Sophia asked. "Some people are happy being single."

"My dad does want a boyfriend. He says so. A lot."

"Do *you* like it when he has a boyfriend?"

"If it's the right person."

"You weren't exactly crazy about his last one, were you?"

"Oh, Nolan!" I exclaimed. "He had such a stupid laugh. Haw, haw, haw. The thing is, my dad just isn't good at picking out boyfriends. It would work better if someone else did it for him. Someone who knows him really well. Me, for example."

"I guess a lot of us could use some help with choosing our partners," Sophia said. "But why do you feel it's something you in particular need to do?"

Our chairs had arm covers made of green fabric. Trying to put together my thoughts, I rubbed one of the covers between my fingers. One side was smooth, the other rough.

"Grace thinks I'm trying to matchmake for my dad because I like to make people do what I want. That may be a little true, but it isn't the main reason. My dad has done so much for me. He rescued me from foster care, which was such a nightmare. I want to give him something back."

Sophia tipped her head to one side. "I can understand that."

"Like we've talked about before, being adopted isn't necessarily a bad thing. You and I know that the people who adopted us really, really wanted kids."

"That's right. People who have their own kids sometimes do it without thinking the whole thing through. That isn't usually the case with parents who adopt."

"My dad really wanted a kid, and he really, really even wanted me specifically. Still…"

"Still…?"

I rubbed the cover some more. Smooth, rough, smooth, rough.

"It's just that—our family is kind of small. There's only one of him, one parent, and one of me, one kid. Next year, I'll start high school. In four years, I'll probably go away to college, or to work. It makes me sad to think of leaving Dad all alone."

Sophia nodded but didn't say anything. I knew this was one of those moments when she was waiting for me to say something. I looked around her office, thinking what that might be. There was the box of tissues on the table beside me in case

I cried, which I did sometimes, and the certificates hanging on the wall that proved Sophia knew what she was doing.

Finally I went on, "I'd never say it to Dad, but when I read a book or watch a movie where a kid has two parents, I feel maybe I'm missing out on something."

"A boyfriend for your dad isn't another parent for you, though. At least not for a while."

"Even at first, a boyfriend would make a nice change. I love my life with Dad, but it is—well, predictable. We usually do the same things at the same time, and usually with just us."

"A boyfriend might liven things up."

"Yeah. The right one, of course."

"And how do you plan to find the right one?"

I frowned, shaking my head. "I don't know. I tell myself I need to be like my cat, Flora, in front of a mouse hole. I need to wait and wait until an idea pops out its head."

After the session, I joined Dad in the waiting room. No matter how busy he was, he always took me to my therapy session, then waited until I was through.

"How was therapy today, sweetheart?" he asked, standing up.

"Fine," I said. "We had a really interesting discussion about my relationship with Flora."

Sometimes I told Dad what I'd talked about in therapy.

And sometimes I didn't.

Chapter 8

To be or not to be? That was the question in my Spanish class one afternoon. Or to put it another way, To be or not to be? What, you can't tell the difference? But it's so obvious.

Mr. Diaz was explaining that Spanish had two words for "to be," *estar* and *ser*. I sighed, trying to wrap my poor little mind around this idea. Why couldn't Spanish just have one word, like good old English? Things must have been so boring in old-time Spain that some Spaniard said to himself, "I know what. Let's have two words for 'to be.' That will make our lives a lot more interesting."

"*Juan está en Costa Rica*,'" Mr. Diaz told the class. "In this case, where you're telling us that Juan is located in Costa Rica at this moment, you use *estar*. '*Juan es de Costa Rica*.' Here, you're describing Juan's place of origin, so instead you use *ser*."

"Where Juan is" versus "where Juan is from." You follow?

I tapped my pencil on my Spanish textbook. At least Mr. Diaz was kind of cute and not ancient, so I didn't mind looking at him. The administration should have made it a rule only to hire teachers who were kind of cute and not ancient. After all, we students had to rest our eyeballs on them for almost an hour a day.

My head was propped up on one hand. I glanced at the clock. It was five minutes earlier than I'd thought. I was dying.

I swung my eyes back to Mr. Diaz. He wasn't just kind of cute, I decided. He was actually a cutie. I checked out his thick black hair and toasty brown skin.

Okay, so my Spanish teacher was a cutie. Big deal. I wasn't going to date him. I leaned the other side of my face on my other hand, just for a change.

Mr. Diaz droned on, in Spanish now, giving me another reason to tune him out. He tried to speak Spanish in class about half the time. A piece of cake for him, since though he was located in San Francisco (*estar*), he was from Puerto Rico (*ser*).

I will *not* check the clock again, I told myself. I knew if I did, I'd find only two minutes had gone by, not a half-hour, which was what it felt like. In which case I'd want to slit my throat. Or someone else's. Or both.

Though I managed not to check the clock, I couldn't help peeking at the calendar on the wall, with its picture of spring wildflowers. May freaking second already. Only twenty days until the anniversary of Dad's parents. Dad still wasn't dating someone, let alone ready to bring him to the anniversary party.

I was running out of ideas for what to do with my mind. Desperate, I focused on all the colors around me. Mr. Diaz wore a purple sports coat, gray shirt, brown leather shoes. The wildflowers in the calendar were yellow. A red, white, and blue flag hung above the door.

Back to the purple sports coat. Mr. Diaz had worn this same coat last week. I'd said to Grace, "Well of course he is, you dingbat. No straight guy is going to wear a purple sports coat."

"You doofus," Grace shot back. "Your mind is a trash can full of dumb stereotypes."

"You knucklehead."

"You numbskull."

"You nincompoop."

This was our latest game, finding rude names to call each other.

Students wondering about their teachers' sex lives—tell me something new. I stared at Mr. Sarudski for an entire U.S.

History class after I found out he was married to Ms. Quinn, the Drama teacher. I could barely imagine them doing the dishes together, let alone doing *it*.

Suddenly I sat up in my chair because—*bang!*—it all came together, like a bunch of math equations.

EQUATION ONE
Purple sports coat
+ Stuff like never mentioning a wife or girlfriend
= Gay

EQUATION TWO
Gay
+ Cutie
= Possible date for Dad

EQUATION THREE
Someone I know
+ Must like kids since he's a teacher
= New boyfriend for Dad who's acceptable to yours truly

I couldn't wait to tell Grace about my fantastic new idea.

Grace wasn't in my Spanish class. She was such a brainiac, she was learning Mandarin, which was ten times harder. I did have her in Gym, my last class of the day.

Since Mr. Alford was out sick, we had a sub, Ms. Delmonico. Ms. Delmonico was a tall, thin twenty-something. Instead of wearing sweats like Mr. Alford, she was dressed in black leggings and a violet top that fell off one shoulder.

"I'll let you kids in on a little secret," Ms. Delmonico said to the class. She held one hand next to the side of her mouth, the way people did when they told a secret. This seemed silly, when she had to talk loudly enough for twenty-three kids to hear. She said, "I'm not actually a gym teacher."

Grace and I exchanged a glance. First rule of subbing: never let the kids know you don't usually teach the subject.

Giving us a ginormous smile, Ms. Delmonico held one arm out to the side and threw the other above her head. "*Dance* is my real field, and my passion."

Another glance. I knew Grace and I would be doing tons of variations on this for the next few days. "*Barfing* is my real field, and my passion."

I had more important things on my mind than our dance-crazy sub. When Ms. Delmonico had the class line up for calisthenics, as usual Grace and I slipped into the back row.

"I found the perfect person," I whispered to her.

"Okay, my budding ballerinas and ballerinos," Ms. Delmonico called out. "Let's start with some shoulder rolls."

Grace: "Who's perfect? Besides me."

Amy: "Mr. Diaz, you turkey. Get with the agenda."

Ms. Delmonico: "Now swing your arms. Let's warm up those lovely arm muscles."

Grace: "Which agenda?"

Amy: "The boyfriend-for-my-dad agenda."

Grace: "Oh, of course. Excuse me for thinking about anything else for even a single second in my entire life."

Ms. Delmonico: "Reach up. Reach in front of you. Make your back a flat table. So flat someone could serve dinner on it, including candlesticks. Reach down to your ten little toes. Come back up."

Amy: "You're excused, if you'll agree that Mr. Diaz is perfect."

Grace: "Mr. Diaz, your Spanish teacher, as a boyfriend for your dad?"

Amy: "Yes! For a smart person, you're sometimes so dopey."

Ms. Delmonico: "Reach down like you're scooping up an armful of flowers. Now—*throw* the flowers into the air."

Grace: "For my dopey sake, let's take this one step at a time."

Ms. Delmonico: "Toe taps next, like you're running in place. Tippy, tap, tippy, tap!"

Grace: "First—is Mr. Diaz definitely, positively, no ifs, ands, or buts gay? You need to nail that down."

Ms. Delmonico: "Please find a partner for everyone's favorite tummy tightener—sit-ups!"

I held Grace's feet. I told her my three equations while she hauled herself up and down. Then Grace held my feet. She popped back an equation of her own.

GRACE'S RAINING ON AMY'S PARADE EQUATION
You aren't actually sure
+ Neither am I
= You'd better find out, which won't be easy

Ms. Delmonico: "Let's do step and clap. Arms overhead. Step to your left and clap. To your right, clap. Woo-hoo, we're partying!"

Amy: "Of course it's easy."

Grace: "Yes?"

Amy: "All I have to do is—"

Grace: "Well?"

Ms. Delmonico: "Exercise is supposed to be fun. Are you boys and girls having fun?"

Some of the kids responded with a blah, "Yeah." One of the smart-aleck boys let out a loud, "No!"

Amy: "I could ask Mr. Diaz how to say 'Are you gay?' in Spanish."

Grace: "Then what? Say, 'Thanks, and by the way, it'd help my Spanish if you'd tell me whether *you* are gay'?"

Ms. Delmonico: "Everyone grab a dumbbell—the real kind, of course, not the person kind! Bend your elbows and swing your arms from side to side."

Amy: "Okay, how would you do it?"

Grace: "I'd bare my soul."

Amy: "'Bare your soul?' Is that a line from some dusty old novel you're reading?"

Grace: "You're pretty sassy for someone who wants my help."

Ms. Delmonico: "Get in as many swings as you can. No dilly dallying."

Amy, not dilly dallying: "All right already, I'll bare my soul."

"That's the idea," Grace said. "Pretend you're baring your soul. But get Mr. Diaz to bare his. Listen, here's how you do it...."

"Hello, you two budding ballerinas in the back row!" Ms. Delmonico called out to Grace and me a few minutes later. "Please open your mouths only to breathe, not to chit chat."

We stopped talking. Fortunately, by now we didn't need to anymore. We already had a brilliant plan all worked out.

Chapter 9

The next day, I asked Mr. Diaz if I could speak with him after school. At three o'clock, I stood back while the students in his Spanish immersion class barreled out of the room, then slipped inside.

Seeing me, Mr. Diaz smiled. "*Hola*, Amy."

For a minute, I thought, "Holy frijole, he's going to speak to me in Spanish. How am I going to do this in freaking Spanish?"

Was I ever relieved when Mr. Diaz said in English, with his cute Puerto Rican accent, "Please have a seat." After motioning me toward a chair, he sat on the edge of his desk, his arms folded.

Mr. Diaz wasn't wearing his purple sports coat today. He wore a sweater instead. I'd heard Dad say something about gay men and fluffy sweaters, I couldn't remember exactly what. They wore them, or used to wear them, or knitted them, or something. I stared at Mr. Diaz's sweater, trying to decide if it was fluffy.

"I'm glad you've come to see me, Amy," Mr. Diaz said. "I hope you don't mind my saying this, but up until now, I haven't felt learning Spanish was the most important thing in your life. Your grade on that last test—well…" He shrugged.

I didn't say anything. I pinched my lips together to keep from complaining about how hard Spanish was, with "Juan is here" versus "Juan is from here" and those dumb accent marks, and, and, and.

"I assume you have a question," Mr. Diaz said. "Is it about the last chapter in our book?"

I ran to the end of the diving board, threw my hands together over my head, and plunged toward a swimming pool five hundred miles below.

"It's like this, Mr. Diaz," I said. "My dad is gay."

His black eyebrows shot up. "I see. Are you having problems with that?"

"No."

"With the other kids at school? Are they giving you a hard time?"

"Oh, you know how kids are. They don't bother me."

"Problems with your other teachers then?" he asked.

After letting myself twirl a lock of hair a few times, I made myself stop. "I had this teacher in seventh grade, Mr. Zimmerman. He told me my father was going to hell, that it said so in the Bible."

Mr. Diaz got up and walked around in the front of the classroom. "Yes, I heard about that incident."

"Do you believe gay people go to hell?" I asked.

"I don't believe anyone does, actually."

"My dad is a good person. He's—he's a photographer."

Mr. Diaz gave me a look that said, *How is that relevant?*

I gave him a look that said, *I'm confused and only thirteen, so don't give me a hard time.* "Anyway, what I wanted to talk to you about is that I think I may be gay too."

"What makes you say that?" Mr. Diaz asked.

I'd worked this part out with Grace.

"Well, I do like boys. But when I'm with my girl friends, for example, my best friend Grace—I don't know, I'm more comfortable. I have a lot more to say to them. And we get a little physical together. You know, goofing around. Grace spends the night with me in my room, in the same bed."

"Girls develop faster than boys," Mr. Diaz said, "physically and emotionally. At your age, you're more in sync with other girls."

"Yeah. That might be it."

Mr. Diaz sat back on the edge of his desk and folded his arms again. "You know, Amy, I'm not an expert in counseling students about this sort of thing."

I tried to make my eyes big and innocent. "No?"

"Wouldn't it be better for you to talk with one of the school counselors, or Ms. Rainier, the psychology teacher?"

"I thought you might—because—"

I was still only three hundred miles into the five hundred mile dive. The swimming pool looked very small down below. I wasn't sure I was going to hit it.

"Because you're Latino," I said. "And my mother is from Guatemala. So we're from the same culture." I didn't mention that my biological dad was African American.

"I see." Mr. Diaz stroked one of his eyebrows. He looked like he was trying to fit together some pieces of a puzzle, but not doing too well. "You chose me to talk to about this because I'm Latino. And maybe because you have an idea that I might be gay?"

I smiled at him. "Yeah."

Mr. Diaz looked me in the eye. "It isn't usually something that comes up in a Spanish class, but, yes, I am gay. Does that make you more comfortable talking about this with me?"

I hit the swimming pool smack dab in the middle. "Oh yes, Mr. Diaz! It does. And I'd love to talk to you more, only—" I shot a glance at the clock. "I have to run now. I'm late for my Journalism Club meeting. Thanks a lot."

I had just a second to see Mr. Diaz's mouth open and his black brows come together, all surprised, before I ran out of the room.

Chapter 10

Next I had to figure out how to bring Mr. Diaz and my dad together. It was easy to get a teacher and a parent to meet if you caused trouble. If you were a (mostly) good kid like me, it was harder.

Grace came up with this plan too. She didn't even say anything, just handed me a brochure.

SUMMER TENNIS CAMP FOR TEENS
AT GREENWAYS COUNTRY CLUB
Ready to improve your tennis game and have fun
with other kids your age?
Then join us!

On the front of the brochure were photos of happy teens on the tennis courts. They chatted together, listened to their coaches, and, yes, even actually hit balls over the net. I didn't have to be as bright as Grace to get what she was driving at. We both knew Mr. Diaz was the coach of the tennis team at Everett.

That evening while Dad was making spaghetti with turkey meatballs for dinner, I gave him the brochure. "Doesn't this sound great?"

"Yes," Dad said, glancing through it. "The only problem is that I can't even afford to buy a hamburger at Greenways, let alone pay for you to go to its tennis camp. Besides, since when have you been so interested in tennis?"

Suddenly I decided to be helpful in the kitchen. I used a wooden spoon to poke the turkey meatballs, which were sizzling in a pan. "You know how kids are, Dad. One minute we're blah about something, the next minute we're all gung-ho."

"Yeah, and soon after I spend a lot of money on some new venture—remember flute lessons?—you go back to being blah."

"You're always saying I'm a natural athlete," I said. "I have good coordination and stuff like that."

Using a fork, Dad pulled some pasta out of the pot of boiling water and tasted it to see if it was done. "Your natural athletic ability doesn't seem to do you much good in Gym, missy. You're barely hanging on to a C. C for 'Could be trying a lot harder.'"

"I might do better in Gym if I had this camp thingy to look forward to."

Dad didn't say anything, just started singing a song from one of his musicals as he drained the pasta. The song was called "Seventy-Six Trombones." He sang it so loudly, it was more like "A Hundred and Seventy-Six Trombones."

I cut in before he got to the second verse. "I realize this program is expensive. But my Spanish teacher, Mr. Diaz, is the tennis coach at Everett, and he knows about some cheaper camps that are just as good."

Dad scratched his beard. "Well, get some other brochures from him and we'll see."

"It might be better if you came to school and talked with Mr. Diaz yourself. It gets kind of complicated."

Luckily, Dad didn't ask exactly how it became all that complicated, because I didn't have any idea.

A couple of days later, there Dad and I were sitting with Mr. Diaz in his classroom after school. Dad and Mr. Diaz together in the same room—I felt like a conductor who had her orchestra gathered together. I just had to lift my baton to start the music.

The only problem was that someone else was in the room with us: Mr. Diaz's student teacher, Ms. Ayala. She was making a display about Spanish words for parts of the body on the corkboard behind the desk where Mr. Diaz sat.

"I agree you don't need to send Amy to somewhere like Greenways for a tennis camp," Mr. Diaz said to Dad. "There are excellent ones at places like Cal or USF that won't cost you a fortune."

Ms. Ayala looked around at Mr. Diaz. "My cousin went to a tennis camp at Cal last summer, and she just loved it."

Why couldn't Ms. Ayala get busy with her corkboard and leave us alone?

"As a matter of fact, I may be doing a mini-camp here at Everett this summer," Mr. Diaz said. "The funding looks iffy, though, so I wouldn't count on it."

Ms. Ayala sighed. "I wonder if I'll ever live to see the day when funding for any school program isn't iffy."

I wanted to snap at her, *We're having a private conversation. Butt out.*

I picked up a framed photo on Mr. Diaz's desk. It showed a dozen kids lined up in front of a tennis net. The one in the middle held a plaque and the others were gesturing toward it, grinning. "Isn't this you with the Everett team?" I asked Mr. Diaz.

"Yes, after we won first place in a local championship."

"You must be a good catch." Oops! "I mean, you must be a good *coach*."

Mr. Diaz smiled. "Some of the kids I've worked with don't think so. They consider me too demanding. According to the grapevine, their nickname for me is Drill Sergeant Diaz. Of course, no one dares call me that to my face, or I'd make him do backhand drills for a half hour."

Mr. Diaz laughed at this, and Dad laughed with him. That seemed like a good sign, that these two were laughing together.

"I'm sure it's hard at times," Dad said, "knowing when to push kids and when to ease off."

Ms. Ayala reached between Dad and Mr. Diaz to grab some more pushpins off the desk. "I resented my demanding high school teachers at the time. Looking back, though, they're the ones I'm most grateful to."

I frowned at Ms. Ayala, then said to Mr. Diaz, "Dad doesn't play tennis, but he does swim."

"Swimming is great exercise," Mr. Diaz said.

"Oh yes!" Ms. Ayala put in. "When you swim, you give every muscle in your body a workout." She gestured at the sketches of a boy and a girl she'd pinned to the corkboard. "*Los brazos, el pecho, las piernas,*" she said, pointing at the different words she was sticking up beside them: the arms, the chest, the legs.

"Isn't it hard to play tennis here in San Francisco?" Dad said. "It's usually so windy."

Mr. Diaz laughed again, his brown eyes sparkling. "If you ever watch me play a match and see me maneuvering to get the downwind end of the court, you'll know why."

I could see Ms. Ayala was about to say something else, maybe about the time the wind blew off her hat, so I jumped in. "Dad, I'm really hungry."

"Are you, sweetheart?" Dad said. "That's okay, we'll be through in a few minutes. We shouldn't take up too much of Mr. Diaz's time."

"Please, call me Enrique," Mr. Diaz said.

"If you call me Travis."

Ms. Ayala opened her mouth again.

I got up and stood in front of Ms. Ayala, blocking her view. "But, Dad, I feel kind of faint and weak. You know how I get sometimes when I haven't eaten."

Dad rummaged in his satchel. "I think I have an energy bar here somewhere."

"Couldn't the three of us just keep talking in the cafe across the street?" I put a stress on *three*. "I really don't feel well."

Ms. Ayala tried to peek around me. "Maybe you should take her home, Mr. McDougall."

I did my best to look like I wasn't feeling so hot, but could still make it across the street. "I only need a bagel or something. Then I'll be fine."

Dad looked at Mr. Diaz. "It's all right with me if—"

"I'm heading out anyway," Mr. Diaz said.

"*Adios*, Ms. Ayala," I said as we were leaving. I wished I knew how to say in Spanish, "Good riddance!"

At the counter in Morning Dew Cafe, we ordered a toasted sesame bagel with cream cheese for me, herbal tea for Dad, and a latte for Mr. Diaz. We sat in a window with a view across the street of Everett's tall white walls.

I nibbled my bagel, which I didn't even want. My campaign was going pretty well. Mr. Diaz and my dad were sitting across from each other, chatting away.

Tennis, blah, blah, blah.

Photography, yah, yah, yah.

The time Dad was hired to take photos of a new line of tennis rackets, nah, nah, nah.

Then Mr. Diaz asked Dad what had made him want to be a father. "Even nowadays, it's unusual for a single guy to become a dad."

Dad shrugged. "I've wanted children for as long as I can remember. When I played house with the neighborhood kids, I'd always take the role of the mom or dad."

Mr. Diaz smiled and took a sip of his latte. "You'd tuck them into bed and tell them a story."

"Exactly. As an adult, I looked into the options, like having a baby with a surrogate mom. But with all the kids who were already around and needing homes, adoption made more sense to me." Dad flicked a finger under my chin. "That's how Princess Bubblegum and I ended up together."

"You make it sound like you two chose each other," Mr. Diaz said.

"We did pretty much," Dad said. "I've always been sure I made the right choice. Amy sometimes wishes she'd held out for a better dad, though."

"That's not true!" I said, slapping Dad's arm.

Usually I enjoyed hearing Dad talk about these things, how he thought he'd made the right choice of a kid and so on. But in my mind, this was Dad and Mr. Diaz's first date. On a first date, they should be talking more about each other.

"You must like kids, too, Mr. Diaz," I said. "I mean, unless someone put a gun to your head to make you become a teacher."

That last part hadn't come out too well. Fortunately, neither Dad nor Mr. Diaz seemed to notice.

"I do like kids," Mr. Diaz said. "I don't have any of my own, but I've got a bunch of young cousins, most of them still in Puerto Rico."

"I've always wanted to go to Puerto Rico," Dad said. "Tell me, what things should be at the top of my list to see there?"

I smiled to myself. Dad and Mr. Diaz were chatting away, and it was all because of me. Was I imagining it, or were they drawing some lines between them, the way people did that day in the museum? Eye lines, love lines, or at least *like* lines.

Later as we walked home Dad said, "So maybe a nice cheapie tennis camp at USF. How does that sound?"

"Fine," I said.

Of course, I didn't have the slightest intention of going to tennis camp. I hated tennis. We'd spent most of the last two weeks in Gym playing tennis, and I'd grumbled about it constantly to Grace. Hitting that darned yellow ball back and forth, back and forth—no thank you very much!

But taking advantage of my status as a dippy teen, I figured I could forget all about the tennis camp idea in a week or two, long before summer.

Chapter 11

What happened next was…a whole lot of nothing. Day after day of Spanish class, and nothing. Day after day at home, and nothing. No phone calls, no dates, nothing from Dad like, "So tell me every single thing you know about Mr. Diaz."

I kept looking for a way to bring Dad and Mr. Diaz together. Finally, I spotted a notice on a bulletin board at school about an Honor Society field trip to Sonoma. Mr. Diaz was one of the supervisors. At the bottom, it said the school needed some parents to go along as chaperones.

Later that day, I found Dad sitting at his computer in the living room. I rested a forearm on one of his shoulders. A lot of times that helped me to get him to do what I wanted.

I told Dad about the field trip. "I really want to go. Sonoma is supposed to be beautiful and—" And what? I racked my brain. "And important in the early history of California. The school says it'll have to cancel the trip, though, if enough parents don't sign up to help."

This wasn't exactly true. In fact, it was completely untrue. Still, the fib was in a good cause.

"Okay," Dad said, "let me look at my schedule and see if I can make it."

Dad just kept scrolling through an article in the *New York Times* about a spacecraft that had managed to go into orbit around an asteroid. I knew I was going to hear some interesting facts about asteroids later.

"Dad," I said, shaking him by the shoulders, "this is very

important and highly urgent. You need to check your schedule now, then call the school first thing tomorrow morning."

Jeez, was I the only one in this family who ever did *anything?*

❧

Thanks to me, Dad checked, and called, and a week later we got on a yellow bus parked in front of Everett. Mr. Diaz was sitting near the front. The seat next to him was empty. Dad said hello to him, then the big idiot kept moving down the aisle with me.

"Dad," I said, "I want to sit with Grace." Grace was waving at me from a seat near the back. "Why don't you sit with Mr. Diaz?"

Dad moved back up the aisle, squeezing past a couple of kids. Just before he reached Mr. Diaz, horrible awful loathsome Ms. Choi, my Earth Science teacher, took the seat next to him. (Actually Ms. Choi was usually pretty cool. It was only at that moment when she was spoiling my plan that she was horrible, awful, and loathsome.) Dad sat next to Mr. Sarudski instead. What good was that, since Mr. Sarudski was married to Ms. Quinn?

"Darn!" I said to Grace. "A golden opportunity lost."

Grace adjusted her glasses. She was always doing that. I didn't see that they ever needed adjusting. "Into every life, some rain must fall." That was called "being philosophical." Also "being unhelpful."

An hour later, we were driving past a green sign that said, "Sonoma, Population 10,648." Big City Girl Amy looked out the window at Small Town, U.S.A.

"There's so much space between the buildings here," I said to Grace. "And so many trees. More trees than people."

"That must be what that sign was talking about," Grace said. "The tree population, not the human one."

I looked at the few people there were on the street, then

around at the multi-hued kids on the bus. "And almost everyone here is so *white*."

We piled out of the bus in front of a long, low building with a red tiled roof. This was Mission San Francisco Solano.

Mr. Sarudski introduced us to three kids who went to a middle school in Sonoma. "Caroline, Brett, and Meg have been trained as tour guides," he said. "They've kindly agreed to show us around." These kids looked like they were from the same family. They all had straight dark-blond hair and blue eyes and dead white skin.

Mr. Sarudski said to the Everett kids, "Now if you would please divide yourselves into three groups…"

Uh-oh, Dad and Grace and I were on one side of the Everett mob, Mr. Diaz on the other. "Come on, you two!" I burst out to Dad and Grace. "We've just got to take a closer look at those incredibly beautiful flowers over there."

I made a beeline for some red flowers that almost brushed against Mr. Diaz's pants. I dragged my dad with one hand, Grace with the other. "Gracie, do you know what these are called? You know a lot about flowers."

Grace squinted at them through her glasses. "These are the Seek-A-Man flower. In the olden days, a woman wore one behind her left ear if she was looking for a boyfriend. Or behind her right ear if she was trying to find a boyfriend for someone else."

I pinched her elbow and whispered in her ear, "In the olden days, they also made a drink from this flower that poisoned people who didn't keep their big mouths shut."

Thanks to my quick thinking, I'd maneuvered us into the same group as Mr. Diaz. This group was led by Caroline, one of the Sonoma kids. We sat with Caroline in front of the mission while she told us about its history.

Caroline seemed nervous at speaking in front of a group and

twisted her hands in her lap. I tried to show her I was listening hard, to make her feel she was doing a good job. When she'd say something like, "Mission Sonoma was the last mission built in California," I'd nod to show I found this interesting.

Sometimes when I talked with a person for a long time and was really focused on her, a funny thing happened. I'd start to feel that I had her face, and that if I spoke, I'd have her voice too. That happened to me with Caroline. After a while, I was sure I had her paper-white skin, her straight blonde hair, her narrow nose, her thin lips. It felt good to imagine we were the same person, the same type anyway.

My eyes shifted from Caroline to a window behind her. In the glass, I saw the actual girl who was looking at Caroline. It took me a few seconds to realize, "Oh, right, that's me."

I didn't look at all like Caroline. Everything about me was different, my hair, skin, nose, lips. I wasn't like Caroline, or those girls I saw in TV shows set in Southern California, who went to the beach all the time and said things like, "I love you, bae," and "Yaaaaasssss!"

While Caroline showed us around the mission, I tried to explain all this to Grace. I liked having a smart best friend, because she did understand, more or less. She said, "Maybe after staring at Amy McDougall for a long time, Caroline felt she looked like *her*."

As Caroline led us through the mission's museum, I didn't forget about Dad and Mr. Diaz. I kept looking for chances to get them to talk with each other. If Mr. Diaz was checking out some Mexican cow hides, I'd haul Dad over there, saying, "Look, Dad, aren't these neat?" Or if Dad was studying a plaque on the wall, I'd say to Mr. Diaz, "Mr. Diaz, could you help me and my dad translate this Spanish?"

The museum had a model showing how the mission looked in the old days. In one corner of the model, a plastic shepherd was herding some plastic sheep. That was what I was like, I thought, herding Dad and Mr. Diaz toward romance. Like Noah, guiding his animals two by two up the gangplank into the Ark.

Nothing much came of all my herding. My attention wandered to other things besides my clueless single dad. Like why had Debbie Parado stopped talking to me? Today she'd sat across the aisle from me on the bus, and when I'd smiled at her, she'd just looked away. Had I offended her somehow?

I missed how Dad and Mr. Diaz got to be looking into the dormitory where the monks used to sleep. I did catch Dad making a gesture with both hands, as if he was talking about moving the wooden beds closer together. Mr. Diaz chuckled.

Yes, I had told Dad that Mr. Diaz was gay. The Amy McDougall Matchmaking Agency was very thorough.

After we'd seen the mission, and General Vallejo's home, and walked around the central plaza, we got ready to head back to the city and more people than trees, and not all white people. I made sure I sat with Grace again, so Dad didn't get any dumb idea about sitting with me.

Success! Because there was Dad and Mr. Diaz getting onto the bus together and sitting next to each other. Ms. Choi had to sit with Mr. Sarudski.

Grace was scribbling away in her chunky notebook. She was the studious sort who took notes about a field trip, when we wouldn't even be tested about what we'd learned.

I gave her a poke in the ribs and nodded toward Dad and Mr. Diaz a few seats ahead of us. I whispered, "Don't forget to make a note about *that*."

Chapter 12

Thursday was Movie Musical Night for Dad and me. We hardly ever got together with other people then. We joked about how Movie Musical Night was "sacred." We wouldn't let anything interfere with it.

We had our Movie Musical Night rituals. First, we put on our matching pajamas. Dad's parents had given us these at Christmas, small size for me, large for Dad. "This way you two can't argue about who got the better present," his mom had laughed.

The pajamas were covered with snowmen and sleds and pine trees. I liked these pajamas because, different as Dad and I looked in most ways, when we wore them, at least something about us was the same.

We cut up apples and made a big bowl of popcorn. Sitting on the couch in front of the TV, we got under the yellow and black afghan Dad's mom had woven for us—another Christmas present. We agreed the afghan was gruesome. Still, it was made with love, so we tried not to spill things on it.

This evening, Flora joined us for Movie Musical Night. She sat on my lap in her meditation pose with her back to the TV. Flora was a fan of afghans and laps and meditation, but not musicals. Unless there was a scene with a mouse, which didn't happen very often.

With Dad's computer hooked up to the TV, we looked for a musical to watch. After a while, we narrowed the selection to three. Dad being Dad, he couldn't make the final decision and instead let me do it.

I chose the musical that sounded the most romantic. A romantic musical might get Dad in a romantic mood about a certain Spanish teacher.

The musical started with two strangers, Jim and Sue, both shopping for wool gloves at a Christmas sale. Only one pair was left in the whole department store. Jim grabbed the right glove and Sue grabbed the left.

Jim and Sue both assumed the gloves were attached to each other, which was true. Also that when they headed toward different cash registers, the other glove would come along with it, which wasn't. Instead, they found themselves holding one of the gloves and some stranger the other.

Jim and Sue sang a song about the gloves.

"I'm sure I saw them first!" Jim sang angrily.

"I will not be coerced!" Sue huffed back.

Then they calmed down and were more polite.

Jim sang, "You should buy the gloves, they really suit you best."

Sue sang, "If you refuse to take them, it will cause me some distress."

By the end of the song, Jim and Sue were all starry-eyed about each other. Together they sang,

> You must take my heart, my love.
> – What is that I'm saying?
> I meant, 'Please take my *glove.*'
> This talk of love's dismaying!

In the end, Jim and Sue bought the gloves together and each took one. They agreed to meet in a couple of days. Whoever couldn't find another pair of gloves to buy would get this pair.

I said to Dad, "I'm pretty sure I know how this movie turns out."

"Yes," Dad said. "He'll marry the saleswoman who sold them

the gloves. She'll marry the doctor who saves her from frostbite because she's running around in winter with only one glove."

I swatted Dad with a corner of the afghan. "Don't be silly."

He crunched into an apple quarter. "All right, all right! The story will end with the two of them walking into the sunset hand in hand. Maybe gloved hand in gloved hand."

"Doesn't that sound nice? Don't you wish something like that would happen to you?"

Dad shook his head sadly. "People walking hand in hand into the sunset happens a lot in movies, kiddo. Not very often in real life."

I shifted around beneath the throw. Not too much, because I didn't want to disturb Flora. Who knows? Could be she was just on the point of getting enlightened.

"Okay," I said, "but you admit it happens sometimes. So why shouldn't it happen to you?"

Having finished his piece of apple, Dad ate a handful of popcorn. "Because I'm too old and cynical."

"You're not all that old—"

"Thank you, Princess Ozma! I'm not *all* that old."

"And if you're cynical—well, you should stop."

"Excellent advice from my young daughter. I should just stop being cynical."

"You're hopeless!" I groaned and slid over sideways on the couch, away from Dad. I startled Flora, who jumped off my lap. She was annoyed, because enlightenment might have been only a paw's length away.

Chapter 13

I mentioned Mr. Diaz to Dad whenever I could. "Mr. Diaz says the imperfect tense in Spanish is really difficult. You remember Mr. Diaz, don't you? You met him at school, and he went on that field trip with us." Things like that. All Dad would say was, "Of course I remember Mr. Diaz. Now about the imperfect..."

We missed the boyfriend-finding deadline of his parents' anniversary party. When it came time for speeches, Dad's mom said, "I just hope all your marriages—and your marriages to come—" (she looked at Dad) "will be as wonderful and long-lasting as mine."

Dad was smiling, but around his eyes, he looked sad.

Dad's parents lived in Arcata, way up the coast to the north. It was a long drive back to San Francisco. Dad and I passed the time belting out songs together, most of them from musicals.

A car was a good place to sing because no outsiders could hear you. Still, sometimes we'd catch funny looks from people zipping past, who could at least *see* what we were doing.

"When is the next big event with your family?" I asked Dad as we rode over the Golden Gate Bridge. "Our family," I corrected myself before he could.

"The annual reunion at the end of September," he said. "That means I've got about four months to become un-single."

I couldn't feel too sorry for Dad. After all, I'd delivered Mr. Diaz to him on a silver platter with an apple in his mouth.

❧

My Christmas present from Grace that year had been a wall calendar with the Chinese character for every month in red. I crossed out each day as it passed. Before I knew it, I'd crossed out so many days that I'd reached the last week of school.

For my crime of being a middle school student, I was sentenced to three days of finals. The worst was Earth Science. At least a lot of it was multiple choice. I'd say to myself, "B is a nice letter, I'll pick B." Or, "I haven't used E much in this column. I'll go with E."

Then came the honest-to-God, actual, very very last day.

Everywhere I went at school, people were signing each other's gold and brown yearbooks. Most people churned out the usual garbage. "It was nice knowing you," "See you next year," "Have a great summer." I tried to be at least a little original when I wrote something myself. "It was absolutely fantastic/completely amazing/truly remarkable knowing you."

In English, nice Ms. Galland gave all of us a present. Small ones, though with a reason for each. Grace got a book of short stories by another Grace, a writer named Grace Paley. My gift was a wand and solution for making bubbles because I'd written a poem about blowing bubbles.

The last-day treat in Spanish was that Mr. Diaz let us do pretty much what we wanted. For me, this was to sit in the back of the classroom and practice my bubble blowing.

I loved making bubbles appear from the tip of the wand with just a puff of my breath. The bubbles gave back wobbly reflections of the world tinted blue, green, red. Each bubble was like an idea. It emerged, floated for a few seconds, then burst.

Through some of my bubbles, I saw Mr. Diaz at the front of the class. He looked like he was inside them. Trying to get him together with Dad, that idea was like a bubble. I came up with it, and it drifted through the air for a while. Then—*poof!*—It was gone.

It didn't sink in until I was walking home—school was actually over. I looked up Church Street and expected to see a big banner.

CONGRATULATIONS EVERETT STUDENTS
YOU'RE ON SUMMER VACATION NOW
HAVE A NICE ONE

There should have been a marching band, too, and people dancing in the streets and throwing confetti. Instead, just the usual things. A streetcar rumbling past. Wind from the ocean shoving the street trees around. People shuffling along like it was any old day.

I had to dance on my own. To skip, mainly. For real dancing, I needed music from the marching band. It was summer vacation, and tomorrow I could blow bubbles all day long if I wanted.

I was excited at dinner. Dad seemed excited, too. At first I thought he might feel this way because I did. Then I realized he had his own reasons.

"Cupcake," he said, "I was thinking we might invite your Spanish teacher to dinner."

I was drinking some water. I was glad I'd finished swallowing. Otherwise I might have spat it all over my plate.

"Mr. Diaz?" I said, my eyes wide. Dad had hardly mentioned him for the last few weeks.

"Yes," Dad said. "Would that be okay with you?"

"Yeah, sure," I said.

"We don't show teachers enough appreciation. Having Mr. Diaz over for a meal would be our way of saying thank you. It seemed better to wait until after the end of the school year, though. That way, no one can claim we bought you a good grade with a pork chop and a piece of cherry pie."

"I understand." Sure, I understood—that Dad wanted Mr. Diaz to come to dinner because he had a big fat crush on him.

"After the summer, you'll be going to Mission High instead of Everett. So we don't need to think of Mr. Diaz as your teacher anymore. There's no reason why I—why we can't all be—well, friends."

"Yeah, sure."

I'd assumed that bubble of mine had burst long ago, the Dad and Mr. Diaz one. But no, it was still hanging in the air, all beautiful and shiny.

ॐ

Dad must have wanted to show Mr. Diaz a big heap of appreciation, because he went to a lot of trouble about that dinner. He got out all his cookbooks and looked at practically every recipe. He went to three stores to shop when usually one was enough.

I looked forward to the dinner as much as Dad. I loved my dad, but like most dads, he was always telling me what to do. Clean your room, do your homework, say please, say thank you. Now it was my chance to run the show. I was the puppet master. I could make not just my dad, but one of my teachers, move when I pulled the strings.

On the day of the dinner, Dad simmered and sifted, boiled and baked, roasted and toasted. I was the underchef. As in "under pressure." Dad was always sort-of-yelling at me things like, "Honey, I need those onions chopped *now!*"

I was sure we'd win over Mr. Diaz with chicken simmered with prunes and green olives. If he managed to resist that, we'd hit him with cinnamon-roasted sweet potatoes. And if even that didn't work, we still had dessert up our sleeve, white chocolate raspberry cheesecake.

Dad was busy in the kitchen until the last minute. When the doorbell rang, he told me to answer it. It was a little freaky at first, to have my Spanish teacher standing in our living room, holding a big bunch of sunflowers. Not in a classroom, holding a smart-board pen.

When I called him Mr. Diaz, he said, "Call me Enrique, Amy. We're on summer vacation." That was freaky, too, the idea of calling him *Enrique.* My solution: not to call him anything.

Dad came into the room. He and Enrique didn't seem sure what to do. Dad held his hands up slightly like he was wondering if he should hug him. The sunflowers were in the way, though.

"These are for you," Enrique said, holding them out. He turned to me. "And for Amy, of course."

"Thank you so much," Dad said. "I love sunflowers."

He gave me one of those Parent Looks that was like a nudge. "Oh, I love them too," I said. "They're just about my favorite."

Dad put the flowers in a vase in the center of the dining table. I moved it a few inches so it wouldn't block Dad and Enrique's view of each other.

Strange. These two had had so much to talk about that time we went to the cafe. They'd chatted away like crazy on the bus ride back from Sonoma. Now while we started eating, they hardly had anything to say.

I looked at Dad. At Enrique. At the sunflowers. I said, "Does Puerto Rico have beautiful flowers, Mr.—Enrique?"

"Yes, very beautiful," said Mr.—Enrique. "Different from here. Tropical, you know."

Silence while we ate our chicken with prunes and olives. Prunes cut in half by yours truly.

I scrunched my face, trying to come up with something else to say. "A lot of your family is still there, right?" I asked.

"Yes," he said. "My mom and lots of aunts and uncles and cousins."

"I'm sorry about the sweet potatoes," Dad said. "I over-cinnamoned them."

Enrique and I assured him the sweet potatoes were perfect. Scrunch, thinking. "Do you miss Puerto Rico?" I said.

"Some things. The beaches. The warm water you can actually swim in."

Dad was still frowning over his dinner. "I apologize that the chicken isn't crisper. Next time I'll put it under the broiler at the end."

The chicken was fantastic, Enrique and I told Dad.

The rest of the dinner wasn't much better. After dessert, I said I was tired and going to bed. Flora came to my room with me, agreeing we should leave the two guys alone. She sat on my pinkish violety comforter and had a meditation session.

After ten minutes, I opened the door a crack and listened.

Dad's voice saying something. Then Enrique's voice saying something.

After another ten, I listened again.

DadandEnriquetalkingtogethersuperquickthensuddenly LAUGHTER.

And after another ten.

Silence.

Not making a sound in my bare feet, I sneaked down the hall to the doorway of the dining room. From there, through an arched opening, I could see the end of the living room with the fireplace. In the mirror above the fireplace, like a picture in a frame, I saw Dad and Enrique holding hands on the couch.

Weird enough to have my Spanish teacher in our apartment. Mucho weird to see him and my dad holding hands there. Still, we matchmakers needed to know these things.

I slipped back into my room and closed the door. Stoked by success, I did a happy dance with my stuffed animals Robbie the Rabbit and Mr. Bear. "Two by two by two by two," I sang, "into the ark they go." I sang softly, so the lovebirds in the living room couldn't hear me.

I would have danced with Flora, too, except she was still meditating.

Chapter 14

The next day over breakfast, I asked Dad, "So did you enjoy the dinner last night?"

"I think it was a success." He looked out the kitchen window over his steaming mug of Morning Thunder tea.

"You had a good time?"

"Uh-huh."

Pause.

"You and Enrique seemed to get along."

"Uh-huh."

Pause.

"Do you think you might want to see him again? You know, on your own."

Finally Dad looked me in the eye, a little sheepish. "Well, as a matter of fact, Amy-kins, I'm seeing him this evening."

"Yes!" I shouted inside my head. Out loud, I just said, "Oh, that's nice."

"Enrique is bringing some food and a bottle of wine, and we're going to watch the sunset over the ocean from Land's End. He wants to take me to a favorite spot of his up on the cliffs."

"That sounds—" I was about to say "romantic," then worried Dad might feel I was rushing things. Expert matchmakers like me knew it was better not to rush things. "It sounds—great," I said.

Sunday, Dad saw Enrique again.

Monday, again.

Tuesday, again.

Soon, Dad was using the word "date." As in, "I'm dating Enrique."

Dad dating Enrique wouldn't be all a bed of roses for me, Grace warned. "You're used to spending a lot of time with your dad. You won't be seeing him as much now that he's dating someone."

I told myself I'd be noble and make sacrifices and share Dad with Enrique. I thought up things Grace and I could do during all those times those two were off somewhere together.

Then a funny thing happened. While Dad was dating Enrique, I saw almost as much of him as before. Only now with Enrique added. Enrique bent over backward to include me in whatever they were doing. Or to include himself in what Dad and I were doing. The three of us went to the movies, to the theater, out to dinner.

"You warned me I wouldn't see as much of my dad," I said to Grace, "but that hasn't turned out to be true. And you know why, girlfriend?"

"I have a feeling you're going to tell me," Grace said.

"Because I chose just the right person to fit into my family. Someone who would make Dad happy, and not make me unhappy by throwing me out into the cold."

"You should give yourself a big pat on the back for being oh-so-smart. You're Amy McDougall, Matchmaker to the Stars. But I have a question for you. Isn't it strange to think about your former Spanish teacher and your dad—?"

Me, already knowing exactly what she was going to say: "Yeah, it is!"

Generally when Dad and Enrique spent the night together, they came to our apartment. Dad didn't want me to be alone there. I wished I could tell him, "Hey, I'd rather be alone than have you guys right here in the apartment while—you know!"

At least Dad's room was across the hall from mine, not next door. I'd lie in bed trying hard to listen, or not listen. The most definite thing I ever heard wasn't moaning or anything like that. Instead, it was Dad laughing his big-guy laugh, loud and boomy.

Grace and I spent a half hour reading a bunch of Yahoo answers to questions like, "How can I get my boyfriend to stop laughing/giggling while we're having sex?" (eleven answers), and "Girls start laughing during sex with me, what should I do?" (four answers).

I learned the answer to another question, why Enrique Diaz never taught first period at Everett. Answer: he wasn't a Morning Person.

Dad and I usually got up at around seven, Enrique at closer to eight-thirty. Most days, I tried to finish my breakfast before he appeared so I wouldn't get in his way. One morning I woke up feeling it was very important I immediately find out everything I could about Justin Bieber's childhood. Had it been mainly happy or kind of sad?

That project took me almost an hour. I was still eating my breakfast when Enrique came into the kitchen. He moved slowly. He looked either sick or old or both. His eyes were only half open.

"Good morning!" I said. I sounded all cheerful. Actually, I was trying to cover up that I felt uncomfortable seeing Enrique in my dad's bathrobe.

Enrique held up one hand so his palm was facing me. I didn't understand the signal.

"Did you sleep well?" I asked.

No answer, except that he held up both hands in the same way.

"It's a nice sunny day," I said. "That awful fog we had for most of the week is gone. That's the one thing I don't like about the summers in San Francisco, all the fog."

Finally Enrique said something, though it was only to croak,

"*No puedo hablar antes de beber mi café.*" Or: I can't talk before I drink my coffee.

This was another reason I avoided Enrique in the morning. For some reason, he reverted to Spanish.

"Dad went to the store to get milk and a few other things. Not the store around the corner, because we've started drinking goat milk instead of cow milk, and he has to go to Whole Foods for that. He read that goat milk is easier to digest. For humans, at least. I guess cow milk is fine for calves."

I was babbling because Enrique made me nervous. He looked inside a bag of coffee by the coffee maker. It was empty.

"*¿Tu papá dijo que iba a comprar café?*" Enrique muttered.

This time, Enrique's Spanish was a little beyond me. When I didn't answer right away, he repeated in English, "Did your dad say he was going to buy coffee?"

I bit my lower lip. "I know he mentioned milk."

"I don't care about the milk, Amy. I care about the coffee."

"Uh, he might have said he was getting coffee too. I'm not sure."

Enrique searched in the cupboards, the refrigerator. After looking everywhere, he leaned back against the counter as if needing some support.

"It looks like you're completely out," he said.

"Out? Oh, you mean out of coffee."

"Yes, coffee." Enrique glared at me, then looked toward the hall. Like he was asking himself: is there any point in trying to get more information out of this stupid girl, should I wait for her father to get back, should I run to the nearest coffee shop?

Just then, Dad showed up. He had bought coffee. He saved Enrique's life by hooking him up to his caffeine IV.

Slipping into my room with my bowl of cereal, I let out a big sigh. Although I would never admit it to Grace, it seemed that matchmaking could have a little bit of a downside.

Chapter 15

I'd scored a bullseye in finding Dad a new boyfriend. I congratulated myself. As usual when I was congratulating myself about something, I wanted Grace to join in.

She did not.

One night, Edith invited Dad, Enrique, and me over for dinner. The adults talked about their plans for the summer.

Edith said, "My plan is to work, work, work. This is the busiest time of year for us landscape designers. I envy you, Enrique, for getting the whole summer off."

Enrique said, "I hate to disillusion you, but teaching is pretty much twenty-four-seven for three hundred and sixty-five days a year."

Putting his hand on Enrique's arm, Dad said, "I've been learning a lot about teachers from Enrique. While they're 'on vacation,' they have to do all sorts of work. Prepare lesson plans for the coming year, learn new technology, network with other teachers."

Chewing on some bean curd in garlic sauce, I tapped Grace's foot with mine under the table. I shot her a look that said, *See how couple-y and supportive Dad and Enrique already are.*

Dad raised his glass. "A toast to Enrique and his fellow teachers, the unsung heroes of our society!"

We toasted Enrique—the adults with wine, Grace and I with water. I gave Grace a second, harder tap on her foot, more like a stomp. Still she didn't respond.

"It's true, I am busy," Enrique said. "Though some time has

opened up in my schedule now that my plans for a summer tennis program have fallen through."

Another tap and look. This time I was saying something different: *Thank goodness! That means he can't try to get me involved in his dumb program.*

Grace put her foot on top of mine to prevent any more taps. She tossed me a look of her own. It said, *Stop pestering me and let me enjoy my Moo Goo Gai Pan.*

As usual, after dinner Grace and I cleared the table and did the dishes. I rinsed them off, and she put them in the dishwasher.

"That's the deal," Edith always said to us. "I cook, and you clean. Any time you girls would rather cook and have me clean, just let me know."

"No, Mom/Edith," we always said. "We like this arrangement just fine."

The wok had to be cleaned by hand, and I scrubbed it with a soapy sponge. "Grace," I said, "when you won that city-wide spelling bee last year, didn't I tell everyone how much I admired you?"

"I seem to remember you said some sort of nice things about me to one or two people."

"When you show me your straight-A report cards, don't I tell you that they're amazing and that you're amazing?"

"Yeah, and you missed some gunk on the bottom." Grace pointed to a spot on the wok.

The adults were still sitting at the table on the other side of the kitchen counter. I lowered my voice so they couldn't hear.

"Then when I find a great boyfriend for my dad, why don't you say, 'Amy, you are amazing too. You're a master matchmaker'?"

"Because for you to call yourself a master matchmaker," Grace said, "you need to make more than one lousy match. Remember that time we were playing baseball in gym class, and I hit the ball clear over the fence and almost beaned some old lady walking past? Did that make me a master baseball player? No. It was just a fluke."

"Gracie, don't you think you're being a little hard on me?"

At that, Grace let loose one of her big beautiful smiles. "Yeah, I am!" she laughed. She flicked some water on me with her wet hands. "That's because my standards for my best friend are super high."

We kept working away at the dishes. I was thinking hard. Finally I said, "Suppose I made another match. What would you think of me as a matchmaker then?"

"A match for someone else?" Grace said. "Who?"

I had no idea.

Then I overheard my dad at the dining table. It was as if he were giving me the answer. He said, "Now it's your turn to get a new boyfriend, Edith."

"That's right," Enrique laughed. "A handsome one, *un novio guapo*."

Edith sighed. "Romance isn't likely to bloom for me at this time of year, only daisies and petunias. As I said, I'm incredibly busy at work."

I looked at Grace. She looked back at me. We communicated telepathically, the way I did with Flora.

"You think you can play matchmaker with my mom?" she half-whispered. "You're crazy!"

"Why crazy? Have you ever tried?"

"No, I haven't. You know me. I believe in minding my own business."

"Oh, come on! Where would the world be if everyone minded his own business?"

"We'd probably avoid a whole bunch of murders and divorces and maybe another world war."

I gave Grace another plate to put in the dishwasher. "What's wrong with playing Cupid for your mom and finding her some nice guy?"

"Are you sure Cupid is a good role model? This wacko baby who runs around shooting people with arrows?"

I pushed up my shoulders in a huge exaggerated shrug. "Okay, Grace. If you honestly believe it's better for your mom not to have a new boyfriend...someone hand-picked by me... probably with your help, if you can spare the time..."

"Well," Grace murmured.

"After you go away to college in a few years, if you think it's better your mom live here in this apartment all by herself..."

Now Grace just made an "ummm" sound. She was weakening, I could tell.

"When she's on her death bed," I said, "if you really and truly feel it's better for her not to have a boyfriend or husband holding her poor shriveled hand—"

Grace rolled her eyes. "All right, go ahead and try to matchmake for my mom. I still think you'll fall flat on your face."

At that moment, Edith bustled into the kitchen. Suddenly I saw her with new eyes. She wasn't just Grace's mom anymore. She was a customer in my budding matchmaking business, though she didn't know it.

Edith was short, like Grace. At that moment, she reminded me of a bird. A pretty bird with shiny black wings/hair. Always bright-eyed and on the go, chirping away.

"Travis and Enrique say they won't leave until I give them their fortune cookies," she said, pulling a plastic bag of them out of a cupboard. "I don't know how I could have forgotten."

One of Edith's traditions at her dinners was to give people fortune cookies at the end, the way they do in Chinese restaurants.

"Come get your fortunes, girls," she told us. She headed back to the dining table with five cookies on a plate.

Grace and I sat back down at the table, and everyone took a cookie.

I almost never liked the fortunes I got in my fortune cookies. I was convinced I had bad-fortune-cookie-luck. I pulled out just enough of the white slip of paper to see the first word of this one. It was *Don't.*

I didn't want a fortune that told me what not to do. I got enough of that already from Dad and teachers, and even from Grace.

"Wait!" I called out before the others had a chance to read their fortunes. "Will someone swap fortunes with me? I have a feeling I'm not going to like the one in this cookie."

"I'll swap with you, Amy," Enrique said. "I'm always ready for a gamble."

Grace said, "You'll be sorry if Amy's fortune says you'll die a slow lingering death, starting in five minutes."

Enrique smiled. "Thanks for the warning, but I'll take my chances."

Enrique handed me his fortune, which was written on a pink slip of paper. I read it out loud. "'If you have something good in your life, keep hold of it.'"

Enrique started to read the fortune I almost got. I wouldn't let him get further than the "Don't." I told him, "I'd rather not know what it says."

"Yeah," Grace put in, "because it may say, 'Don't worry, you'll win a million dollars in the lottery.'"

I decided the "something good in my life" was Dad. Of course I wanted to keep hold of him.

"I like my fortune best," Grace told us. "It says, 'If you're still hungry, eat more Chinese food.'"

Chapter 16

Dad had already given me the idea of matchmaking for Edith. On the ride back to our place, he and Enrique handed me some more ideas.

"It shouldn't be that hard for Edith to find guys to date," Dad said to Enrique. "Most of her co-workers at her design firm are men."

"And she must meet a lot of men through her projects," Enrique said. "Contractors and stonemasons and tree-pruners and people like that."

I rubbed my chin. I thought, Edith's firm... Meeting a lot of men through her projects...

I snapped my fingers. As in, Eureka, I've got it!

Over the next couple of days, Grace and I worked out another of our brilliant plans. One evening when I was at her place, we put it into action.

Grace and I washed up as usual after dinner. As for Edith, she cleared a space at the dining table and opened her laptop.

I nudged Grace to get her attention, then nodded toward Edith. Grace knew what I had in mind.

"What are you doing, Mom?" Grace asked.

"I want to put in a little more time on one of my projects from work."

"Can we take a peek?" I asked.

"Sure." We stood behind her, looking at the screen. "We're landscaping that new elementary school that's going in by Lake Merced," Edith said. Using her mouse, she flipped through some of her plans and drawings.

We chatted with Edith about the project. Whether she should plant bamboo along this wall or boxwood and things like that. Then I said, "You know, Edith, this reminds me of something Grace and I have been meaning to talk to you about."

"Yeah," Grace said. "Since we're starting high school soon, we're trying to do some serious thinking about what careers might interest us."

"That's an excellent idea," Edith said.

"Ms. Galland told us about something called the Day-in-the-Life approach," Grace said.

"You find a person with a job you might like," I explained, "then you ask if you can spend the day with her."

"You know," Grace said, "go to where she works and see what she does, and think about whether you could stand doing it yourself if you got paid enough money."

I communicated through my eyes to Grace: *You're not helping.* To Edith, I said, "I love to draw, and I know you do a lot of drawing in your job."

"And Amy and I both love plants and nature and all that sort of thing," Grace said. "So we thought we should look into landscape design."

"It would be super fantastic if we could experience a Day in the Life of Edith Kwan," I said. Behind my back, I had my fingers crossed for good luck.

Edith didn't respond right away. She was still studying one of her drawings on the screen, zooming in and out on it. I worried she'd tell us something like, "I'm flattered, but I'm just too busy."

At last she said, "I'd be delighted to have you girls tag along with me for a day."

I gave a sigh of relief and thought I heard Grace give one too.

Edith checked her calendar. "How about tomorrow?"

So far, so good.

❧

In the firm where Edith worked, all the designers sat at desks in one big open area. "This layout is great," I said to Edith, looking around. I meant it was great for matchmaking, because I could see everyone who worked there. No one could hide from the keen eyes of Amy McDougall, Master Matchmaker.

I spotted one guy who seemed like a good potential boyfriend for Edith. About the right age, not bad-looking. He was carrying a big plastic watering can and a feather duster.

I went over to him while Edith was showing Grace some plans at her desk.

"Hi there," I said.

"Hi," the guy said. He showed nice white teeth in a nice big smile. He poured water from his watering can onto one of the indoor plants.

"I guess you landscape design people really do love plants," I said, "because gosh, here you are looking after one right in your office."

He frowned at me. "I don't understand." Now I noticed he had an accent.

"This is beautiful." I rubbed one of the leaves of the plant between my fingers.

"Yes," the man smiled, "very beautiful." He dusted the leaves with his feather duster. "In the Yucatan where I come from, these grow wild, in the jungle."

"What is this plant called?"

Again he frowned. "Sorry, I don't understand. My English isn't so good."

Now I was the one who frowned and didn't understand. "You do work here?"

"Work here?" the man said. "Yes. Each Tuesday morning, I come and occupy myself of the plants."

I saw Grace beckoning me. When I went over to her, she

whispered, "I hope you aren't thinking of getting my mom together with Jose from the plant care company who can hardly speak English."

I tried for a save. "They say that's the best way to learn a foreign language, to have a boyfriend or girlfriend who speaks it."

"My mom already speaks Mandarin and English," Grace said, "and doesn't have any plans to learn Spanish too. So you'd better get your rear end in gear and find someone more appropriate."

I pinned my hopes on the guys we would meet at Edith's work sites. One site was an apartment complex, another a shopping center, the third, the backyard of a big house. Grace and I agreed to try to chat with the guys working at each place.

At the apartment complex, Edith introduced us to the first guy we came across, Marty.

"Marty is an expert in grass," she told us. "I call him the Grass King."

"Oh really," I said. Grace and I had to pretend to be interested in all the landscaping stuff. That was our cover.

Edith went to check on how the workers were coming along with a retaining wall. Grace and I stuck with Marty. Grace said to him, "So you know all about grass."

"I sure do, kid," he said. "That's why I'm here today, to give your mom some expert advice. Look, I'll show you."

Opening the back of his pickup, Marty pointed at what looked like a square of shaggy green wall-to-wall carpeting. He ran his hand over it like he was petting it, the way I pet Flora. "This grass is called Empire Zoysia." With his fist, he whacked another square lying next to it. "This other is St. Augustine."

Marty turned to Grace. "Your mom wants to use St. Augustine in this project. But I keep telling her, 'No, Edith, you'd be much better off with Empire Zoysia.' I brought along these two samples to help me convince her."

"Gee," I said, looking at the two pieces of wall-to-wall

carpeting, "you must get a lot of mud and dirt on your boots working with grass. When you go home, does your wife or girlfriend or boyfriend or whatever get mad at you for tracking in?"

Marty chuckled. "Well, Amy, I don't have a wife or girlfriend or boyfriend or whatever, so it's not a problem. The only one waiting for me at home is my dog Bruiser, and I don't think he cares all that much if I get the place dirty."

"And you never have had a wi—" Grace started to say.

"Let me tell you girls more about Empire Zoysia," Marty cut in. "This baby can grow in both hot and cold climates. Because of its massive root structure, it doesn't need as much water as most grasses."

Marty's incredibly fascinating lecture about Empire Zoysia went on and on. The grass was low maintenance, resistant to insects and diseases, and a beautiful bright green. "Empire Zoysia is the grass of the future," Marty assured us.

Marty put his hand on Grace's shoulder. "I sure wish you'd talk to your mom about all the good features of Empire Zoysia. It really is—"

"We know," Grace said. "It's the grass of the future."

We found Edith at the retaining wall. She asked if we'd enjoyed chatting with Marty.

"He seems really nice," Grace said.

"Do you like him, Edith?" I asked.

"I love Marty, he's such a great guy." That was promising. Then Edith added, "Too bad he's the most boring man on earth. I can never get him to talk about anything except grass, grass, grass."

I crossed Marty off my mental list of boyfriend prospects. Not a problem, because there were lots of other guys to investigate at this site, and two more sites to go after that.

In fact, there were so many guys, I got out my sketchbook and made drawings of them to keep them all straight. I added trees and flowerbeds to throw people off the scent if they saw what I was doing.

Grace took notes in her chunky notebook. Only instead of saying things about landscaping, she wrote, *Sam, carpenter, age thirty-nine, single, likes sailing and jazz.*

During the drive back to Edith's place at the end of the day, Grace and I mentioned one guy after another we'd met at the work sites. Mixed with a lot of talk about landscaping, so she wouldn't get suspicious. Edith had reasons for pooh-poohing every guy. Marty was boring, and this man was obnoxious, and that guy wasn't very bright. There was always something.

"I told you this wouldn't be easy," Grace said when we were alone. "My mom is hyper picky when it comes to dating."

"She did marry your dad," I said, "so it isn't that she never ever picks. All we need to do is find some more candidates."

"Do you have any bright ideas about where to look?"

I bit on one of my knuckles. Sometimes this helped me think—and sometimes, like now, it didn't.

"No," I admitted.

Our matchmaking hopes perked up when Edith invited us to one of her business networking events. That is, until we found out it was organized by a group called Women in the Workplace.

Edith said, "I think you two will be inspired to see a big group of businesswomen getting together, with hardly a man in sight."

Grace and I couldn't come up with a good reason not to go to the event after all our talk about our potential careers. So we went.

A hundred or so women filled a big conference room in a hotel downtown. They talked with each other, and munched on finger foods, and exchanged business cards. A woman named

Teresa made a speech about how she'd started her own business selling vintage clothes on eBay.

I was sure what Teresa was saying must be interesting, but I couldn't understand her very well because the sound system created an echo. What I heard was, "Now-ow-ow I have-ave-ave a multi-ti-ti-million-ion-ion-dollar-ar-ar empire-ire-ire with my-y-y own-own-own clothing-ing-ing line-ine-ine."

Along with the hundred or so women at the event there were exactly three-count-them-three men. I managed to talk with all three and ruled them out one by one. The guy who was there with his wife, the guy who'd come with his girlfriend, the gay guy accompanying a woman friend.

At least the finger foods were tasty. Grace and I stood by the table where they were laid out and grazed. We had a scintillating conversation that went like this:

"The onion dip is yummy."

"Have you tried the hard-boiled eggs?"

"There's only one cheese puff left, you'd better grab it."

That was Grace warning me about the last cheese puff. I wished she'd also warned me to eat it in two bites rather than one, because when a man and a woman arrived late at the event, I was distracted by having my mouth stuffed with cheese puffiness.

My talk with Grace now went like this, in low voices:

Amy: "He's the right age."

Grace: "Check."

Amy: "At a business meeting, which means he might be a good match for Edith."

Grace: "Check."

Amy: "Don't you think he has a certain—something about him?"

Grace: "Certainly a certain something."

Amy: "Who's the lady with him, though?"

Grace: "We'll have to find out."

Fortunately, the man and the woman came over to the table and started putting food on their plates.

"Let me guess," the man said. He pointed at Grace. "You're a vice president at Google." Then at me. "And you're the founder of a multinational corporation with offices in New York and London." He flashed a dazzling smile. "How about it, girls? Am I close?"

Grace and I giggled. I wondered whether this guy was as perfect as he seemed for the job of dating Edith. After he told us his name was Brian Anderson, he even helped by saying, without our even having to ask, "And this is my sister Roz."

"This is his sister, Grace," I said, relieved. Not his wife or girlfriend.

"Yeah," Grace said, "I heard him."

Roz smiled at us and shook hands. "I'm glad to see you two are getting an early start on your climb up the career ladder."

Brian dropped his voice, as if to say something confidential. "I know that as a mere man, I really shouldn't be here. But the friend Roz was planning to come with got sick, and we didn't want to waste her ticket."

"And your wife or girlfriend or boyfriend or whatever" (I needed to find a shorter way of saying that) "could get along without you for the evening?"

"I'm very single at the moment," Brian smiled, "so luckily it wasn't a sacrifice for anyone."

Single. Yes!

Brian said, "I promised Roz that if she let me come to her almost-all-women's event, I wouldn't talk about myself and my business with anyone, only about her and her business."

"But we want you to talk about yourself!" I blurted out.

Brian laughed, making his green eyes sparkle. I hoped Edith had a thing for green eyes.

"Great," he said, "because I love doing that. I run a chain of print shops called Perfectly Perfect Print. We print business cards, among other things. How would you girls like a coupon for a hundred free business cards?"

Brian gave us each a coupon. "There's something in it for me, naturally. When you're handing out your cards, people will say, 'What a nice card,' and turn it over and see 'Printed by Perfectly Perfect Print.' What do you two business experts think of my marketing idea?"

"I think it's just fantastic," I said. "We should introduce you to Grace's mom, Edith. She's the pretty lady over there in the black dress. At least I think she's pretty."

Brian aimed his green-eyed gaze at Edith. As if feeling it, she turned in his direction, though we were too far away for me to be sure she was looking right at him. Were these two making an eye line together? A like line, an I-want-to-know-you line?

"I agree," Brian said. "She is pretty."

"I'm sure she'd enjoy talking with you," I said. "She's a landscape designer and a very interesting person."

"She and my dad are divorced," Grace said. "Which means she's single, too."

I telepathed to Grace, *Don't be too obvious.*

"I'd be happy to meet your mom," Brian said.

"I would too," Roz said, "but first I need to grab a few minutes with a couple of women I know over by the window."

Grace and I introduced Brian to Edith. I hoped it would be like those times in a movie where the two people on the screen looked at each other and I would know they'd fallen in love at first sight. In case I didn't get the message, the soundtrack would nudge me, usually with the help of a lot of violins.

It wasn't like those scenes in the movies, but at least Brian and Edith seemed to enjoy talking with each other. Brian said some things that made Edith laugh. Edith said some things that made Brian nod his head, looking interested.

I thought it was better if Grace and I didn't hover. Good matchmakers tried not to hover. Instead, we returned to the food table, though we did keep an eye on Edith and Brian.

"They're still talking to each other," I said to Grace after a while.

"Yeah," Grace said. "People are supposed to be networking, but there only seems to be one net those two are interested in working."

Edith was chatting with Brian right up until the moment the three of us left. I waited until we were sitting on the streetcar before I said to Edith, "You and Brian seemed to hit it off."

"Yes, I guess we did," was all Edith said.

"I wouldn't mind seeing him again," Grace said. She paused, then added, "Do you think that might happen, Mom, that we see him again?"

Edith ran a hand over her glossy black hair. "I don't know about you, but I'm seeing him tomorrow for lunch. My firm has a lot of print work, and Brian may be able to help us with it."

Grace and I didn't look at each other. We didn't need to. I knew we were both thinking, *You don't have lunch with someone just to talk about some print jobs.*

I had to wait five whole days before I heard any more news. At last one afternoon, I got a text from Grace. *It's official. Brian and Mom are dating. Who-ray!*

I remembered that coupon Brian had given me for free business cards and filled it out. Where it asked for my name and profession, I wrote:

Amy McDougall,
Master Matchmaker.

Chapter 17

Soon after Brian started dating Edith, he invited us all—including Dad and Enrique—to a pool party at his place.

Brian lived in Woodside, a town south of San Francisco. He lived in a small house on a big piece of land. The house was old and painted yellow and a little rundown. The land was pretty, with lots of big trees, but all tangled and overgrown. Brian was so neat and tidy himself, I was surprised his house and land weren't that way too.

Grace and I changed into our swimsuits in a storeroom that stuck out of the back of the house. This room was so stuffed with old furniture and junk, it was hard for us not to bang into something while we got into our swimsuits.

"What's that weird sound?" Grace said, turning her head.

I listened. "Some kind of animal."

When we'd finished changing, we investigated. We found a half-dozen chickens fenced into the corner made by the storeroom and the main house.

As a couple of city girls, we stared at the chickens. They were milling around and scratching at the dirt.

"I can't remember the last time I saw a real live chicken," Grace said.

"Neither can I," I said.

"Why do you think Brian has chickens?"

"I don't know. Why did the chicken cross the road?"

"No one has ever been able to figure that out."

Brian had invited some adults to the party with kids who

were about the same age as Grace and me. We kids spent most of our time in the pool. We played Marco Polo and other games, or just splashed around.

At one point, Grace and I were resting our heads on our arms at the side of the pool. We could see Brian and Edith over by the barbecue. Edith put her straw hat on Brian, and he put his round cloth one on her. They laughed.

"Brian and your mom sure seem to get along," I said.

"It's fantastic," Grace said. "My mom is so happy."

I watched Dad and Enrique for a few minutes. They sat in deck chairs, their heads tipped back.

"I'd love to live somewhere like this, out in nature," I heard Enrique say.

"That's a great fantasy," Dad said, "but you couldn't live here without a car."

Enrique looked over at him. "I forgot about that! What would I do without you to talk common sense into me?" He smiled and took Dad's hand.

Another success story.

"Now do you admit I'm one of the greatest matchmakers the world has ever known?" I asked Grace.

I assumed she would say, "Of course, and I apologize for ever doubting you."

Instead, she said, "Well, you didn't exactly make that match with Brian, did you? I mean, he and Mom were both at the same event, and they'd probably have met even if you hadn't been there."

I looked at Grace with the most shocked and horrified expression I could manage. "I...don't...believe...my...ears. You're trying to say I did not make that match?"

"If you'd known Brian was going to the event and arranged for my mom to go, too, that would be real matchmaking."

I didn't argue. What was the point when someone was being

completely unreasonable? But I promised myself I'd make that persnickety Grace admit I was a Matchmaker Extraordinaire.

The chance for this came sooner than I expected. At least a maybe-chance. We got chummy with Carla, one of the other kids. She went to Everett, too, and I knew her by sight. Grace and I complained to her about how slow our social lives had been so far this summer.

"School can be a drag," I said, "but at least it throws us together with a lot of other kids our age."

"I'm going to one of Jerry Silva's famous parties on Saturday," Carla said. "I can probably snag you two an invite. That might give your social life a boost."

"No, thanks," Grace said. "I've heard about Jerry's parties. Playing Truth or Dare, and answering lots of embarrassing questions, or being told to crack an egg on your head and dumb stuff like that. Not my thing."

"Grace," I said, "I think we should go. What else will we do on Saturday night? Play Monopoly again?"

I reasoned and kidded and coaxed Grace until she agreed to go to the party with me.

Because I had a brilliant new plan.

Jerry Silva had what you needed for a good party: the right place and the right parents.

The right place was a backyard that sloped down a hill so neighbors couldn't see what your guests were doing on the flat strip of lawn near the bottom. The right parents were ones who thought all they had to do when their son gave a party was be at home, even if they were watching a movie in the living room. Not actually go out in the yard to see what the kids were up to.

Even if the parents had come snooping, at first the party looked pretty innocent. The sun wasn't going to set for another hour, so there was plenty of light. Some of us sat on garden furniture or a redwood log, others on the grass. We munched on chips and nuts and drank soft drinks.

Only soft drinks. Drinking booze wasn't what Jerry's parties were famous for. They were famous for their party games. And for "things happening." The gossip was fuzzy about exactly what "things" happened. All I knew for sure was that this was where some big Everett romances had gotten started: Deanna and Joel, Marco and Kaylee.

My brilliant plan was to get Grace together with one of the guys there. I'd come to the party not sure how to do the getting together. I'd just have to improvise.

"We're not playing Truth or Dare this time," Jerry told us. "I'm bored with that. Instead, we're going to play a game I invented called Kiss and Tell."

Kiss and Tell. That sounded promising.

Jerry had the six boys line up wearing blindfolds. A scarf, a towel held together with a safety pin, things like that. Jerry would tap one of the girls on the shoulder, and she'd start down the line, kissing the boys. "Only dry kissing, people," he told us. "No tongue action."

I thought, *Yes, please. I'm not ready for that.*

After a girl had kissed all the boys, they slipped off their blindfolds long enough to "tell." In other words, write their guess about who it had been on a notepad.

As I watched the other girls take their turns, my eyes were wide. If I kissed six boys at the party, it would be about as many as I'd kissed until now in my whole life. I didn't count having Lucas Patterson for a sort-of-boyfriend for a few months in sixth grade. Despite a lot of sitting close to each other during lunch hours, he'd never actually kissed me.

It was my turn. To help me cope, I took it one kiss at a time.

Approached the first boy, Anthony Broussard.

Leaned forward.

Kissed.

After a few seconds, I got that it was mainly up to me, the girl, to decide how long the kiss should last. I didn't want to make it so short that it was insulting. On the other hand, I didn't want to make it so long it seemed like I was getting carried away. I guessed at the right length as best I could, then moved on to the next guy.

After the last girl had gone down the line, Jerry checked the boys' answers. He announced that Denry Amaral had gotten the most right. Jerry gave Denry a strawberry-flavored lip gloss as a prize. "To keep your lips soft for all that kissing you must do," he joked. Denry applied the gloss to his lips and puckered them, clowning around.

Denry Amaral. That was interesting.

I took a long look at Denry. He was mixed African American and Anglo. He had beautiful loopy black hair and toffee-colored skin. I said to Grace in a low voice, "Don't you think Denry is the cutest guy here?"

"Denry? He's not bad-looking. Such a big nerd, though."

I stared at Grace with wide, disbelieving eyes. Who was she to write off some guy as a nerd? She was such a big nerd-ess herself.

"I actually think Denry is primo boyfriend material for you." There, I'd planted the suggestion.

"Denry? The only things Denry is interested in is practicing his clarinet for Band and dazzling his math and science teachers. Not girls."

"Shh," I whispered. "He's looking at you."

Denry smiled at Grace, his teeth very white against his darkish skin. I was pretty sure an I-like-you line shot between them, like a laser beam.

"And now it's the girls' turn to guess," Jerry told us. "After this round, I'll give two prizes. One for the girl who gets the most right answers. The other for the girl who gets the least. Because clearly that girl needs to improve her kissing skills.

Denry Amaral, our winner in the first round, will give her a private Kiss and Tell lesson!"

Opportunity knocked. I tried to think how to open the door.

Jerry handed out the blindfolds and notepads. At the top of my pad, I wrote: *Grace*.

The lips of the first boy who kissed me were sort of full. Probably Binyam. After he'd finished going down the line, I wrote on my pad: *1. Ivan*.

I could smell something sweet and flowery on the next guy. Ivan's hair products that we teased him about? I wrote: *2. Binyam*.

Once we'd kissed all the guys, Jerry asked for our scores. The girls handed their pages down the row toward Jerry. I was next to Jerry, but instead of passing them to him, I begged, "Oh, Jerry, please let me change my answers." I didn't wait for a response. Instead, I started making a new list on my pad, with my own name at the top.

I kept talking. "Once I'd kissed all the guys, I realized I'd made a couple of mistakes. I always do better on tests when I re-do them like this at the last minute. Why, on my Algebra final, I got a B minus after re-doing it, when I'm sure I would have failed otherwise."

In the meantime, almost everyone was shouting at me and protesting, though in a jokey way. After all, who really cared if I did the test over?

After adding my new Amy score to the pile, I found Grace's real one. Pretending it was my old one, I took it out and stuck it in my pocket.

After checking the girls' answers, Jerry announced, "The winner of this round of Kiss and Tell is—Yvonne!" Jerry gave Yvonne a Super Stay coral-orange lipstick. She laughed, putting it on her lips.

"Last place goes to"—Jerry pointed at her— "Grace Kwan!"

Grace's jaw dropped. She wasn't used to getting the lowest score on any kind of test, even a Kiss and Tell one. The other kids made a sound that was a blend of "ah!" and "ooh!" and "ha!"

Jerry said, "All right, Grace, it's time for your private kissing lesson."

Grace shrank back, stammering, "But I'm not sure…"

"Of course you are," I whispered. I gave her a good strong shove toward Denry.

"You've only got ten minutes, Denry," Jerry said, "so make it a crash course. I want you two to head over to the corner of the yard behind the bamboo. I'll blow my whistle when your time is up."

While Grace and Denry headed around the bamboo, the other kids made an even bigger "ah-ooh-ha!"

We chatted and ate more snack foods. I stared at the screen of bamboo but couldn't see anything. I tried to hear something from behind it, but couldn't, with all the noise the kids were making.

After ten minutes, Jerry blew his whistle. Grace and Denry reappeared. The kids made lots of teasing remarks. Grace and Denry didn't say a word and tried to look like absolutely nothing had happened behind the bamboo.

I waited until Dad picked us up and Grace and I were sitting in the back seat of the car. Then I said to her in a low voice, "I'm dying to know. How was your kissing lesson with Denry?"

"Fine," was all Grace said at first. After a few seconds, she added, "I guess practicing the clarinet gives you a lot of lip control."

I nodded, taking this in. "Did you give him your number?"

"Yeah."

"Are you seeing him again?"

95

"Yeah, tomorrow."

I held out her old test score.

Grace peered at it through her glasses. "What are you doing with—?" Then she understood.

I had a pleased-with-myself look on my face. "So what do you say, Grace? Am I or am I not?"

"Are you or are you not what?"

I handed her my new business card.

Grace gave a laugh, seeing the name of my profession underneath. Then a few more laughs. Then she was laughing out of control, rocking backward and forward, and so was I.

Chapter 18

Dad and I were just a little family of two. Still, we had our family traditions. For Valentine's Day, we decorated the apartment with paper cut-outs of hearts and Cupids. On Halloween, we put on costumes and joined the crowds on Castro Street. And every year on the Fourth of July, we went to Dolores Park to watch the fireworks over the Bay.

Usually Grace and Edith joined us. This year we brought an even bigger group. Thanks to little old me, Dad, Edith, and Grace had boyfriends, and they all came along.

This was the first time I'd seen the three couples together. As we walked to the park, I tuned into their different conversations. First, to Dad and Enrique's. They were ahead of me. Dad carried his mini barbecue, Enrique a lot of the food. Suddenly Dad stopped in his tracks.

"Oh my God," he exclaimed, "I forgot to bring mustard and ketchup for the tofu burgers!"

"Don't worry," Enrique said, "I grabbed them on the way out."

A few steps farther on, Dad stopped again. "What about napkins?"

"They're in my backpack."

Dad looked at the box Enrique held against his chest. "Make sure you keep the cheesecake upright. Otherwise the strawberries and blueberries and white frosting will get smooshed together, and instead of a cake with red, white, and blue, we'll have nothing except purple."

"The cheesecake is doing very nicely."

Dad smiled at Enrique. "How did I cope on the Fourth of July before I met you?"

"I sometimes wonder."

I smiled to myself. Those two were getting along just fine.

Next, I focused on Edith and Brian, who were behind me. Edith was carrying a small American flag. I could hear Brian say to her, "It looks like you're all set to celebrate the Fourth. You can wave your flag during the fireworks."

Edith laughed. "It's not a good idea to tell me when to wave this flag, Brian. It was given to me at my swearing-in ceremony to become a U.S. citizen. They showed us a video of the president greeting us and beautiful pictures of America. They told us to wave the flag—but I didn't."

"I'm deeply shocked, Edith," Brian said. "Weren't you proud to become an American?" I could tell he was joking. Brian was usually joking.

"Of course I was," Edith said. "But for me, being American was about making my own decisions, not just doing what I was told. And my first decision as an American was not to wave this flag."

I looked around in time to see Brian kiss Edith on the cheek. "I love people who march to a different drummer," he told her.

That couple seemed to be doing well, too.

Next I turned my attention to Grace and Denry, who were walking beside me.

Grace was saying to Denry, "Wouldn't it be fascinating to travel back in time to July Fourth 1776? We could see the Founding Fathers sign the Declaration of Independence."

Denry stuck out his chin a little. He did this right before he tried to impress people by saying something uber-intelligent. "You can't travel back in time," he told Grace. "The laws of physics make it impossible."

I rolled my eyes. Denry was always saying nerdy things like, "The laws of physics make it impossible," or explaining why dinosaurs became extinct, or what terrible things would happen if you fell into a black hole.

"I could go forward in time, though, couldn't I?" Grace said. "Have a Fourth of July celebration with my great-great-great grandchildren?"

"Yeah," Denry said, "if you made a round trip to earth traveling in a spaceship that moved at close to the speed of light."

Grace pushed her glasses up her nose, mulling this over. "Would I be all wrinkled and ancient by the time I got back?"

"As far as you were concerned, you'd only have aged in normal time. From the point of view of people on earth, though, you'd be hundreds of years older."

Behind her glasses, Grace's eyes had stars twinkling in them. Love stars.

"You're so smart, Denry," she sighed, "and you know the most interesting things."

I was glad someone thought they were interesting. Since I didn't so much, I changed the subject. I said to Grace, "Isn't it exciting to think we're going to Mission High in September?" We were passing one side of Mission High School, which faced Dolores Park.

To my surprise, Grace looked embarrassed. She sneaked a glance at Denry that seemed almost guilty.

"Grace, I think we should just be honest with Amy about the issue," Denry said. He turned to me. "I keep telling Grace she shouldn't go to Mission High. She ought to go to Lowell like me."

Lowell was a magnet high school in San Francisco where lots of the smartest kids went. I hadn't even tried to get in myself. My grades just weren't good enough.

"Grace has everything she needs to get into Lowell," Denry said. "I don't understand what's holding her back."

"I've explained to you, Denry," Grace said. "Mission High is a great school too. It's closer to where I live, and a lot of my friends from Everett are going there."

"I know," Denry frowned. "But I'm not."

Grace got all coy and flirty. "Are you saying it matters to you that we won't be going to the same school? That after the summer vacation, you'll miss seeing me every day?"

Normally Denry was so articulate. Now he stammered, "Well...I mean...you know...you see..." At last he came out with, "Yeah, if you really want to know, I will miss you."

"Oh, Denry!" Grace exclaimed. She put her arm through his. The love stars in her eyes twinkled even more brightly.

Things seemed a-okay with Grace and Denry.

As the three couples crossed the street, I trailed a little behind, like a proud Noah shepherding his animals into the ark, two by two.

Part of Dolores Park was on the side of a hill. This was San Francisco, where lots of things were on the side of a hill. If not on the side, then on top. To get the best view, we joined the crowd at the highest section of the park.

Grace and I had brought a couple of blankets, and we spread them on the lawn for our group to sit on. Although the sky was almost dark, the lamps in the park gave us plenty of light to see by. A little buzz of excitement ran through the crowd as we waited for the fireworks to start.

Looking around at my group, I felt my own buzz. I, Amy McDougall, had turned these six single people into three happy-so-far couples. I wanted to wave Edith's flag and yell at the people around us, "Look at me! Aren't I incredible?" I wanted to turn to smarty-pants Denry and say, "I may not know as much as you about the laws of physics, but I know a lot more about the laws of love."

Dad grilled tofu burgers for us on his barbecue. He handed me one on a bun. "You seem to be in a very good mood, Amycakes."

"Do I?" I smiled.

"I have some great news for you. It's such great news, I almost wish you were in a bad mood, because it would snap you right out of it."

I put ketchup on my tofu burger, then mustard, then relish, then a bit more ketchup. "Are you buying yourself a new computer? Which means I can have your old one, which at least isn't as old as your even older one that I'm using now?"

"No, no. You're very cold."

"We're going to spend the entire month of August in Paris in an apartment with a view of the Eiffel Tower?"

"No. Still cold."

"You're going to send me to the Art Institute next summer so I can jump-start becoming a famous artist?"

"Warmer. My news is about learning, though not something art-related. And not something you do sitting down."

I took a bite of my tofu burger. "Not about art. Not about something I do sitting down... I give up."

Dad gestured at Enrique. "The world-famous tennis coach Enrique Diaz has agreed to share his vast knowledge of the game with you."

The happy look of a person who was about to get a marvelous surprise was still stuck on my face. After a few seconds, it melted into more like *Say what?*

"Amy," Dad went on, "remember how back in May you told me you wanted to go to a tennis camp this summer? You didn't mention it even once after that. Still, I knew that was just you not wanting to be one of those Gimme kids. You know, the kind who are always saying to their parents, 'Gimme, gimme, gimme!'" Dad held out his hands, flexing them in a gimme, gimme gesture.

"Oh well," I mumbled modestly, looking down at the blanket.

"I blame myself for never getting off the dime and signing you up for a camp. Then a couple of days ago, I was talking to Enrique about the camp idea, and he dreamed up something even better."

I took another bite of my tofu burger. I wanted to have something to do with my face besides looking worried and confused. "You mean, to give me a tennis lesson himself?"

"Not a lesson, Amy."

"Sorry. A few, then?"

"A whole series. Enrique is going to create your own summer tennis camp experience, right on the courts at Everett Middle School. Enrique, show Amy the schedule you made."

Beaming proudly, Enrique handed me two calendar pages, one for the rest of July and another for the first half of August. Every Monday, Wednesday, and Friday, my name appeared next to "2:00-4:00 p.m." For each of these days, he'd written things like *racket control* and *basic footwork drills*.

"That's wonderful!" Edith exclaimed, looking at the schedule over my shoulder.

"Why, by the end of the summer, you'll be a real tennis champ," Brian said.

I didn't say anything. I pretended I wanted to be polite and finish my bite of tofu burger first.

I did sneak a glance at Grace, who was sneaking a glance at me. Grace knew I hated tennis. She knew the last thing in the world I wanted was to take tennis lessons three times a week for the rest of my summer vacation.

"Enrique has refused to accept a cent for your lessons," Dad said. "Isn't that generous of him?"

By now I didn't have anything left in my mouth to chew. I had to say something. "Tennis lessons. You mean, with a bunch of other kids?"

"No, private lessons!" Enrique exclaimed. He had a look on his face like he was telling me I'd won a trip around the world.

Denry said, "I'm taking private clarinet lessons this summer. Believe me, Amy, you'll make a lot more progress that way."

Dad was starting to look worried about my reaction. He rubbed his beard nervously. "I expected you to be thrilled, Amy."

Grace said to me under her breath, "You'd better stop hiding your intense excitement."

At that moment, fireworks started going off above the Bay. They splashed against the dark sky like big flowers made from colored light. Somewhere nearby, firecrackers exploded. It was as if everyone were celebrating this super fabulous thing that had just happened to me. Celebrating my Dependence Day, when I lost my freedom for three afternoons a week for the rest of summer.

"Amy, did you have your heart set on a real tennis camp?" Dad said. "Is that the problem?"

"But, Amy," Enrique said, "working one on one will give us a chance to get to know each other better."

"Amy, it's such a great opportunity," Brian said.

"I wish I'd had a coach give me tennis lessons when I was your age," Edith said.

"You don't want to waste your whole summer doing dumb things like watching videos on Netflix, do you?" Denry said.

Actually, I did, though I wasn't about to admit it.

Grace just looked at me. Her eyes asked, *So what in the world are you going to say to them?*

What was I going to say? Would I be a brat? Tell them I

refused to play tennis anywhere except in a camp with other kids? Admit I considered tennis stupid and boring?

I looked at the six pairs of eyes fixed on me. I took hold of a lock of my hair and gave it a few nervous twirls. After a minute, I said, "The whole plan sounds—just fantastic."

Chapter 19

Later that evening, Grace sat on the edge of my bed. I got down on my knees in front of her, clasping my hands. I begged her to please, please, please tell Dad and Enrique she was dying to take tennis lessons with me.

Grace was so cruel. Her answer was, "No. No way. Absolutely not."

"You can't leave me to take lessons with Drill Sergeant Diaz all by myself," I said. "If you take them with me, there'll be someone else for him to catch doing dumb things and yell at. That would at least give me some breathing space."

"Throwing yourself at my feet won't change my mind, so you might as well get up." Grace pulled at my forearms, making me stand.

"I don't like tennis any more than you do," she said. "Besides, I want to spend as much time as I can with Denry before school starts and we're torn asunder, like Romeo and Juliet. Only by feuding schools, not feuding families."

"Oh, Denry!" I muttered. "You wouldn't even be involved with him if it weren't for me." I plopped down next to Grace on the bed. It made a loud squeak. "Grace, these tennis lessons are like our taking gym class together. Remember how last year I juggled my schedule around so I could be in the same class with you?"

"Don't give me that! You wanted gym class that period because that's when Floyd Porter was taking it, and you had a humongous crush on him."

I bit my knuckle, trying to think of other angles. "What if I paid you to have lessons with me?"

"How much?"

I pretended to look shocked. "Grace, you'd actually take money from a friend for something like that?"

"Only if there were plenty of it, which I seriously doubt."

Picturing the thirty-seven dollars and something cents in my piggy bank, I dropped this approach too.

After that, Grace refused to talk about the subject anymore. She kept her mouth closed and pinched down at the corners. That was when I knew I was in trouble in an argument with her, if she wouldn't speak to me. How could I go on arguing with someone who didn't even say anything?

The flaw in Enrique Diaz's Summer Tennis Camp for One was that it didn't have any flaws. At least not from the parental point of view. Dad didn't have to pay for it, and he didn't have to worry about me traveling a long way to get there. All I had to do was walk seven blocks to Everett, like I'd done the whole school year.

Enrique was waiting for me at the front entrance. He wore white shorts, polo shirt, shoes, and socks. Even his cap was white.

"All set for your first private tennis lesson, Amy?" he asked.

"Yeah, sure," I said, while thinking, *No, not really.*

Enrique put a hand on my shoulder, moving me forward. "Just think. This could be a day you'll remember for the rest of your life. After a fantastic start to your training by moi, you may go on to become the next Steffi Graf or Serena Williams."

I thought, *I may go on to become sick to my stomach.*

In the big asphalt yard behind the school, we had one of the two tennis courts to use without waiting. In fact, with Everett in summer school snooze mode, we could have used both courts if we'd wanted, switching back and forth. For that matter, we could have raced around the whole yard bashing tennis balls, except in the basketball court at the other end, where some guys were shooting hoops.

Enrique walked up and down in front of me the way I'd seen guys do in war movies in front of their troops. Drill Sergeant Diaz and his troop of one: me.

"Tell me, Amy," Enrique said as he paced, "what has your experience of tennis been so far? Stand up straight. Good posture off the court gets you ready for good playing on."

I jerked my body upright. "Only as a quick part of the program in gym class. You know, somewhere between badminton and folk-dancing."

"What made you think you wanted to learn more about it? Shoulders back, Amy. Both feet flat on the ground."

I threw back my shoulders and stopped shuffling my feet.

I said, "Well, I enjoyed the little bit I did play." Complete lie. "And it seemed more fun than some other sports." Yeah, like alligator wrestling.

"Personally," Enrique said, "I believe tennis is the greatest sport there is. If you're a competitive person like me, it's an excellent outlet. Unless you're playing doubles, it's also an individual sport. If I lose a match, I can't blame my team members. On the other hand, if I win—which I prefer to do—I get all the glory. So tell me, Amy, would you like to become a winner at tennis?"

I was about to call out, *Yes, sir!* and salute, the way soldiers did in war movies. Then I thought better of my little joke. "Sure," I said.

"Excellent! I know you're probably dying to start playing, but first we need to warm up."

Enrique had us do side shuffles, lunges, and high knees. High knees involved jogging around the court lifting my knees as high as I could. It was my least favorite exercise. Naturally, that was the one Enrique wanted to do the most.

"Get your knees up, knees up, knees up!" Enrique called out, jogging behind me. "Come on, Amy, don't be a lazy bum. You can do better than that. Knees up, Amy McDougall. Higher. Higher!"

Oh God, I thought, *this is only getting ready for tennis. Not even playing it.*

At last Enrique handed me the racket he'd brought for me. I sneaked a look at my phone. We were only fifteen minutes into a two-hour lesson.

We worked on my forehand. Enrique yelled to me from the other side of the court, "Keep your eye on the ball, Amy! Bend your knees! Get your racket up!"

At least those were commands I understood, even if I couldn't always follow them. Other ones just confused me. For example, when Enrique told me not to hit the ball.

"What do you mean, 'Don't hit the ball'?" I called back over the net to him. "Isn't that what tennis is all about?"

"I mean you don't want to hit it over the net so much as just push it over, punch it over, touch it over."

"Okay," I said. "That's perfectly clear."

And when I pushed, punched, or touched, Enrique said I shouldn't use my arm.

"What should I use then, my head?" I called to him.

"Think more about swiveling your feet and engaging your stomach, not so much about swinging your arm."

Enrique had me running all over the court, chasing those darned yellow balls. I panted. My heart banged against my rib cage like it wanted to escape. The ponytail I'd made that morning kept flopping against my sweaty neck.

While Enrique did give me some breaks for water, he ended them after only a few minutes. He'd grab my water bottle away from me and exclaim, "I know you're just dying to get back on the court!"

Finally, Enrique said the best thing I'd heard from him during the whole lesson: "Okay, Amy. That's enough for today."

While we crossed the yard, Enrique asked how I felt.

"My right arm is sore," I said, rubbing it.

"I told you, you're putting too much force in your swing."

"And I have a headache."

"That's because you aren't used to exercising. Kids are getting more and more sedentary. The human body wasn't designed for sitting around, though. Our early ancestors spent most of the day on the go."

"Their tennis game must have been fantastic," I muttered.

Before I said goodbye to Enrique in front of the school, I tried to think of something polite to say about the lesson. That took a little doing.

"It seemed like we covered a lot of ground," I told him.

Enrique looked surprised. "You think so? I didn't even start on the backhand, which I do in the first lesson if the student is a quick learner."

Hauling my exhausted body toward home, I knew the words they'd write on my tombstone.

AMY McDOUGALL, NOT A QUICK LEARNER

Chapter 20

Thanks to Enrique, I had a new fabulous-not summer schedule, with three afternoons a week gobbled up by tennis lessons.

On Wednesdays, my lesson ended at four o'clock and my therapy session started at four-thirty. Dad would pick me up at Everett and rush me over to Sophia's office in my sweatpants. I wasn't too happy about being rushed during my summer vacation, and I felt scuzzy sitting across from Sophia in sweatpants, maybe even with some sweat still on them.

Before I started the lessons, I would talk to Sophia about all sorts of different things. Afterward, I pretty much had only one topic: how much I hated tennis.

Two weeks into July, I sat in the green armchair, angrily swinging my right leg back and forth. "I keep thinking these lessons will get easier," I said. "I'll learn the basics, I'll improve. Instead, they just become harder. I have to learn more and more new things. In the meantime, I'm supposed to hold onto all the things I already know."

Sophia nodded. "Learning something new like tennis is hard, isn't it?"

"Enrique is pushing me more with every lesson. He calls me on any little mistake I make."

Sophia tipped her head to one side in that way she had. "You're really not enjoying these lessons at all?"

"Only when I make a great shot to Enrique and he flubs his return."

"Enrique said one purpose of the lessons was to give you

two a chance to spend some time together. How do you feel about that idea?"

"I feel like I'm seeing more of him than Dad these days, and that was not part of the plan. When I do see Dad, I'm usually seeing Enrique too, because whatever we do, he wants to do it with us."

"You did say you hoped finding your dad a boyfriend would liven things up for you two. Perhaps you got a little more liveliness than you wished for."

I frowned at this. If a friend told me she was going to start seeing a therapist, the first piece of advice I'd give would be: *Don't tell your therapist anything you don't want her to remember forever.*

Suddenly I realized I hadn't told Sophia about my accident.

"Look what happened to my knee today." I stopped swinging my leg and pulled up my sweats to show the bandage. "I fell down on the court."

Sophia leaned forward to study my knee. "Do you think it was Enrique's fault you hurt yourself?"

"No," I admitted. "My right foot tripped on my left."

"Did you go home afterward?"

"No. I cleaned off the scrape with some water and my towel." This wasn't sounding as dramatic as I would have liked. I tossed in, "I'm sure that towel is ruined."

"And you went on playing? With your knee scraped?"

"Enrique gave me a bandage."

"I'm wondering why you didn't end the lesson. You say you don't enjoy them, and you had the perfect excuse."

I sighed and played with the zipper of my hoodie. I wanted sympathy not a cross-examination. "I guess—well, at that first lesson, Enrique said he was competitive. I'm realizing I'm competitive too. I have fantasies of winning lots of gleaming tennis trophies someday. Also of trouncing Drill Sergeant Diaz. Maybe in a few years when I'm sixteen and he's thirty-seven and over the hill."

My mind jumped to something else. "I'll tell you another thing. Not everyone likes Enrique."

"Someone you know doesn't like him?"

"Not a someone exactly. More like a something. Flora, my cat."

Sophia raised her eyebrows, making her eyebrow ring lift up slightly, too. "Oh yes, Flora."

"If Enrique comes into one room, usually Flora goes into another. If she does stay, she either ignores him or gives him one of her dirty looks. You know cats. They're experts at dirty looks. One day I asked Flora why she didn't like him."

My eye caught on one of Sophia's certificates on the wall, reminding me she was a health care professional. "I mean, I imagined asking her," I corrected myself. Though Sophia and I got along well, there was always a chance she'd have me locked up if she thought I was truly psycho.

"And what did you imagine Flora answered?"

"That she didn't like Enrique because he was a dog."

"A dog?"

"You know, a dog type of person."

Sophia nodded and said, "I see."

When I got home, I took out my sketchbook and pencils. I drew a picture of Enrique as a dog. A dog body with Enrique's face.

A particular type of dog. The kind who was always there every time I turned around. Nuzzling me, looking at me, demanding attention. The kind of dog I wanted to tell, "Can you please just leave me alone for five minutes?"

Flora sat on the bed, watching me with her jade-green eyes half closed. I held up the drawing in front of her. "Is this how you see Enrique?" I asked.

Flora opened her eyes wider. Her triangular ears twitched. She said, "More or less."

At least, I imagined that was what she said.

Chapter 21

I complained to Sophia that Enrique didn't give Dad and me more alone time. Whenever I felt I wasn't getting enough, I reminded myself, *We always have Movie Musical Night.* At least that one night a week was our time. Dad and Daughter Time.

At any rate, it was until that Thursday.

Dad asked, "Amy dear, would you mind if just this once Enrique joined us for Movie Musical Night?"

Dad only called me "Amy dear" when he felt guilty about something.

"I couldn't see him yesterday evening because I was helping Janet hang some pictures," Dad said, "and we can't get together Friday because he has an event with his men's doubles team. And he says MMN sounds so fun, with eating apple slices and popcorn and all."

I opened my mouth and even got out the "yeah" in "Yeah, I do mind." I stopped myself. I could tell I wouldn't like the way it sounded. Petty. Selfish.

Instead I said, "Yeah, I guess that would be okay. Just this once."

That night, the three of us sat in front of the TV, ready to pick a movie. Dad and I didn't wear our matching pajamas with snowmen and pine trees. Dad had worried Enrique would feel left out because he wasn't wearing the same thing.

Dad sat between Enrique and me. With the three of us using it, the ugly afghan only reached far enough to cover one of my legs. Flora boycotted the whole business in disgust, despite the lure of wool and several laps to choose from.

"I'm happy to see whatever movie you two want," Enrique said.

"Amy and I usually watch a musical," Dad said.

I glared at him. "What are you talking about? We always watch a musical. This is Movie Musical Night, for heaven's sake."

I'd forgotten about not wanting to seem petty and selfish.

"That's fine," Enrique said. "Though frankly, I'm not crazy about musicals. You know, people are talking, and it's like real life. Then the orchestra starts playing, and the actors are singing and dancing, and you realize it's all phony baloney."

I looked at Dad, and he looked at me.

Dad stroked his beard. "What about *West Side Story*? That involves Puerto Ricans, so it should be interesting for you."

"Oh, please, with the lead Puerto Rican played by this Russian-American girl in dark make-up? We could watch that new Argentinian comedy. That would be good for Amy's Spanish."

"Amy, is that all right with you?" Dad asked.

"Okay," I said. Dad was always telling me to be polite to guests, and I was doing my best.

Enrique started to search for the movie. "Of course, we should watch it without subtitles."

I sat through what might have been a simply high-larious film, except I couldn't understand more than one in ten of the words people were spewing out. Dad, who hadn't studied Spanish in years, probably understood even less. We didn't sing along to any songs because there weren't any.

I did get that the movie was a rom com. Felipe and Luis were both in love with Isabella.

At one point, Isabella accidentally invited both Felipe and Luis to dinner on the same evening. Felipe asked her what she was making. She said something I didn't understand. Then Luis said something in response that I also didn't understand, but that made Enrique explode with laughter.

Tired of trying to follow the Spanish, I closed my eyes and invented my own scene.

FADE IN:

INTERIOR OF AMY-BELLA'S KITCHEN, NIGHT

AMY-BELLA, wearing an apron, stirs a steaming pot on the stove. Dashing, seductive FELIPE CABEZA DE VACA Y PICASSO and dark, smoldering LUIS DE SANTA TERESITA DEL NIÑO JESÚS glare at each other suspiciously through the steam.

FELIPE
Amy-bella, what are we having for dinner?

LUIS
Yes, Amy-bella, what are you making us?

AMY-BELLA
I'll show you!

AMY-BELLA whisks off her apron, revealing a black leotard underneath. An orchestra starts a zippy number, and the walls of the kitchen slide away to reveal a steaming pot the size of a barn silo.

Amazing dance routines follow between AMY-BELLA and men dressed as a TOMATO, an ONION, a GARLIC CLOVE, and a CHICKEN. AMY-BELLA'S slow dance with the GARLIC CLOVE is especially amazing.

The music becomes faster and louder. With AMY-BELLA pointing the way, all the men/food items climb a spiral ramp and dive into the steaming pot. Their expressions show they're happy to sacrifice themselves for the sake of a tasty meal.

FELIPE and LUIS
Gosh, Amy-Bella, can't you ever give a simple answer to a simple question?

If I couldn't watch a freaking musical on what should have been freaking Movie Musical Night, I'd at least freaking fantasize one. At the end of the movie, Enrique asked what we thought of it.

"It was cute," I said. Since I'd barely understood most of the movie, I thought that was what was called a "diplomatic answer."

"I liked all the shots of Buenos Aires," Dad said.

I wondered if Dad was being diplomatic too.

"Isn't the guy who played Felipe great?" Enrique said. "His name is Santiago Turati."

"Actually," Dad said, "I thought the guy who played Luis was a better actor."

"Oh no, Turati is much better. He's a big star in Argentina."

"That may be, Enrique. I still think the other guy is more talented."

Enrique rolled his eyes, as if to say, *Of course you're wrong, but I won't keep arguing with you.*

He leaned toward me over Dad. "How did you do with the Spanish, Amy?"

"I understood some words," I said. Like *the* and *with*.

Enrique munched on the last of the apple slices. I wanted more of these myself. If I'd known Enrique would eat so many, I'd have cut up another apple.

"Next movie night," he said, "we can watch the same movie with subtitles. You'll pick up a lot of what you missed this time."

"But Enrique—" I started to say.

"*¿Qué es, muchacha?*"

Dad said, "I thought I explained, Enrique. Thursday evenings are generally a chance for Amy and me to have some time together by ourselves."

"And they're Movie Musical Nights," I said. When was he going to get that straight?

Enrique looked at me, then at Dad. His mouth was a bit open in surprise. His brown eyes looked a little sad and hurt.

"I'm sorry. I guess I didn't understand. You mean every Thursday evening?"

"Obviously not every single Thursday," Dad said, "because you're here this evening. But usually."

Enrique reached for another apple slice on the plate. Looking down, he found there weren't any more.

Chapter 22

I complained a lot to Sophia about Enrique and even more to Grace. Grace joked that I was a newspaper, the *Daily Complainer*. When I complained, she'd say, "Is that what it says today in the *Daily Complainer*?"

The one person I hardly complained to was Dad. Enrique was a gift I'd given him. After presenting the gift, I didn't want to say, "Are you sure you like it? Sure you don't want me to take it back? Sure you can't see all its flaws?"

I figured I'd let Dad handle his relationship with Enrique, and I'd handle mine. We'd keep them in separate, water-tight containers. And we did pretty much, until the day I was looking everywhere for my violet hoodie. That day, my container sprang a leak.

I loved my violet hoodie. I was convinced its shade of violet looked fantastic with my coloring. That morning, I couldn't find the hoodie in my room. I'd worn it the day before. Could I have left it on a bench beside the tennis court at Everett? Or at the Eureka Valley branch library, where I'd gone afterward?

Searching for the hoodie had made me late fixing my breakfast. A few minutes after I entered the kitchen, Enrique came trudging in.

Seeing Enrique in the morning, it was hard to believe he'd be full of energy later, bashing tennis balls across the net. His shirt was partly tucked in, partly out. He looked at me with eyes that weren't completely open.

"Where's my coffee?" was all he said. Not, "Good morning,

Amy darling, how are you, did you sleep well?" Usually Dad had Enrique's coffee ready for him when he got up. Not this morning for some reason.

"I thought I had him trained," Enrique mumbled, starting to make it himself.

I was about to take some food out of the cupboard. I asked myself if I should escape to my room instead and come back later. But I wanted to find out if Enrique remembered my having my hoodie when we left Everett.

I only got out, "Enrique, I wanted to ask you if—" before he cut me off.

"*Disculpe*, Amy." Then he said something in Spanish that I was pretty sure meant, *The part of my brain that communicates with other human beings isn't working yet.*

The part of his brain that spoke English didn't seem to be working either.

"I just have a quick ques—"

Enrique snapped, "No."

"I only wanted to ask if you'd seen—"

"And I only want coffee. Glorious, all-powerful, life-enhancing coffee."

I slammed the cupboard door, making the box of rice puffs inside fall over. Enrique didn't seem to notice. I headed for the back porch. He hardly noticed that either. He was watching his coffee drip into the glass pot like it was a magic potion.

I rushed down the back stairs of the building. I could have gone to my room but didn't like being penned up there while I was angry.

Reaching the yard, I found Dad lying on his back on the bench. He had his camera pointed at the banners of fog racing by overhead. I was always stumbling on Dad taking pictures of things. The light on the living room walls, clouds out the window, bugs or flowers in the yard. That was life with a photography nut.

Sitting up, Dad turned his camera on me. "You look as mad as a wet hen. Did Enrique growl at you? You should know better than to speak to him before he's coffee-d up."

As he talked, Dad kept taking pictures of me, *click click click.* I had my arms crossed and was scowling.

"Why can't he—?" I began.

"Why can't he what? Be a nice sensible morning person like you and me?" *Click click click.*

I asked, "Isn't it better to have a boyfriend with the same, well, rhythms as you?"

"I read a study about that recently in the *New York Times.*" Dad pointed his camera at me. *Click.* "But if that's true, why did you go and matchmake us, Princess Tam Tam?"

I froze. "I didn't—"

"Or perhaps you weren't aware of your Spanish teacher's rhythms."

"I never—"

"Of course not," Dad laughed. "I was only pulling your leg. No, Enrique and I meeting, that was one of those lucky accidents."

I breathed a sigh of relief, though I tried to make it inconspicuous. "You still think it was lucky?"

"Of course," Dad said, putting down his camera. "In case you haven't noticed, I'm crazy about Enrique. He's smart, enthusiastic, responsible, and kind of cute besides. How does the accident look from where you sit? Lucky or un?"

I pouted. "It doesn't matter what I think."

"Sure it does. I don't want to be involved with someone you don't like. Especially since..."

I narrowed my eyes suspiciously. "Especially since what?"

Dad sighed. "I was going to wait to discuss this with you until the details were clearer. But I guess now is as good a time as any. Enrique's landlord plans to make some renovations to his building. Enrique will have to move out of his apartment temporarily. We're not exactly sure when."

My eyes went from narrow to wide. "And you want to ask him to move in with us?"

"It does make sense. He's over here a lot anyway, because I want us to be around for your sake. And we live only a fifteen minute walk away from Everett."

My thoughts spun round and round. "How long is 'temporarily'?"

"A month or so."

When our own landlord had rebuilt our back stairs, that was only supposed to take "a week or so." Instead, it took more like three.

I said, "Are you telling me you're going to invite him to live here, or are you asking me if it's okay?"

"If you say absolutely, definitely not, then Enrique will just have to find another solution."

Dad looked at me with his blue eyes. His blue eyes that I'd heard people say were his best feature. His eyes that were so unlike my own brown ones. I was already almost sure I couldn't look into those eyes and say, "Absolutely, definitely not." Still, I struggled a little longer.

"Dad, I like Enrique. But he can be, well, kind of bossy."

Dad laughed. "That's true."

"And a know-it-all."

"Pumpkin, he's a teacher. It's his job to be a know-it-all."

"And intrusive. I'm sure he's going to try to horn in on more of our Movie Musical Nights."

Dad chuckled. "I wouldn't put it past him. But doesn't that show he wants to make himself more a part of our family?"

Dad and I sat quietly on the bench for a few minutes. I looked up at the fog streamers shooting past. I told myself summer would end soon, and those heinous tennis lessons would too.

School would start for both Enrique and me, and we'd be busy and probably not at home all that much anyway.

Finally, I said, "Okay, Dad. You can let Enrique stay with us. As a guest. Temporarily. Temporarily underlined, in bold and italics and a big font."

Dad put his arm around my shoulders and hugged me. "That's my generous, big-hearted girl. I'm sure we'll all get along together really well."

Different words danced through my own head. *That makes one of us.*

Chapter 23

That evening, Enrique came to dinner. While Dad was serving the lentil soup, he brought up that Enrique needed to move out of his place soon.

"Amy and I would be pleased if you'd be our guest here," he said.

Dad swung his eyes over to me, giving me my cue. I said, "Yeah, Enrique, you're welcome to stay with us."

I looked at Dad, giving him a cue of my own. "Temporarily, that is," he added. "Until the work is finished on your building."

"That's so nice of you both," Enrique said. His brown doggy eyes were shining, as if we'd just offered him a delicious bone. "Of course, I couldn't impose on you."

"You wouldn't be imposing," Dad said.

"You're over here so much as it is," I said, "it's like you're already staying here."

Dad shot me one of his disapproving looks. He turned to Enrique. "What Amy means is, all the signs are that we could make a smooth transition."

"I don't agree," Enrique said. "It's one thing for me drop by here, another for me to be a long-term guest."

I froze with a spoonful of soup halfway to my mouth. Was it possible Enrique wouldn't come to stay with us after all?

Then Enrique said, "The only way I'd feel comfortable accepting your offer is if we first had a trial."

"A trial?" Dad said.

"Yeah. I could stay with you for, say, a week right away, and then we'd see if it would work for me to stay longer once the renovation gets going."

"But—" I struggled to come up with an objection. "Why not wait until the renovation starts, then come here, and that first week would be the trial?"

"Because if things didn't work out, where would I go in that case?"

I had to admit that was logical.

Enrique started his trial week with us that Friday. The news made the headlines of the *Daily Complainer*, which I emailed to Grace.

THE DAILY COMPLAINER

Sunday, July 31

SAN FRANCISCO. Residents of Duboce Avenue had a shock today when Enrique Diaz moved into the erstwhile peaceful home of Travis and Amy McDougall.

The crowd watching the move-in gasped with disbelief at the large number of items Mr. Diaz transferred from Mr. McDougall's car to the McDougall home.

When questioned by our reporter, Mr. Diaz said, "You know how it is. You pack about as much stuff for a short trip as you do for one around the world."

Reporter: "Mr. Diaz, I'm sure our readers would like to know why you felt it necessary to bring along your own coffee maker. My sources tell me there's already a perfectly good one in the McDougall household."

Mr. Diaz: "The McDougalls' coffee maker lacks many features of my Latissima Perfecta Pro. This adds the exact amount of sugar I like, stirs the finished product for me, and even tells me, 'Ummm, this coffee smells great, I'm sure you'll enjoy it.'"

Reporter: "Mr. Diaz, have you given any thought about the ways your stay with the McDougalls may be inconvenient and disruptive for them?"

Mr. Diaz: "No."

Comments: 1

Grace Kwan, 2 hours ago: "This so-called news article is just a shameless plug for a Latissima Perfecta Pro. How dumm do you think us readers is?"

THE DAILY COMPLAINER

Monday, August 1

SAN FRANCISCO. The Association for the Investigation of Paranormal Activity and General Weirdness received a panic-stricken call today from a Ms. Amy McDougall, who claimed her home was inhabited by a poltergeist.

"For the last two hours, it's been making strange banging and humming and inhaling noises throughout the whole apartment. I'm scared out of my wits!"

Ms. Clare Voyant from the Association urged Ms. McDougall to open the door to her room and look outside. "That may help you fathom these mysterious goings-on."

Several tense minutes later, Ms. McDougall came back on the line. "Following your advice, I've discovered that the source of the strange noises is our house guest, Mr. Enrique Diaz."

"Your house guest?" Ms. Voyant queried. "Not a polter-guest?"

"No. Mr. Diaz said he wants to do my dad and me a favor by giving the apartment a 'clean and fluff.' I told him our cleaning lady had been here just a couple of days ago. He said, 'I'm sure I'm much more thorough.'

"I asked Mr. Diaz how much longer he'd continue making noise, because I wanted to take a nap. My cat Flora telepathed the same message, though a lack of cat-telepathic-sensitivity may have kept him from receiving it.

"Mr. Diaz gave a big smile and said, 'You can't hurry the perfect cleaning job.'"

Comments: 1

Grace Kwan, 52 minutes ago: "This paper has stooped to a new low in this sensationalistic story about the paranormal. My ghost friend Herbert agrees with me."

THE DAILY COMPLAINER

Tuesday, August 2

SAN FRANCISCO. Startled neighbors reported a piercing shriek coming from the McDougall home early this evening. Breaking down the door to the apartment, police came upon the cowering figure of Ms. Amy McDougall.

"It's in there!" Ms. McDougall exclaimed, pointing down the hall.

"What is 'it,' young lady," the officer asked, "and where is 'there'?"

"'There' is our dining room,'" sobbed the distressed, yet also strikingly pretty and bright Ms. McDougall. "The 'it' is pork feet with garbanzo beans, with actual nasty, icky pigs' feet bobbing in a blood-red tomato sauce."

"And who perpetrated this revolting dish?" the officer inquired.

"Our house guest Mr. Diaz insisted on making my dad and me a genuine Puerto Rican dinner. He said this would help him repay us for our hospitality."

"I'm afraid I'll have to take in Mr. Diaz and book him," the officer said. "San Francisco takes culinary crimes very seriously."

In the police station, the officer brought several charges against Mr. Diaz, including:

A-sauce and Buttery;

Disturbing the Piece of Pie; and

Disorderly Cooking

Comments: 1

Grace Kwan, 15 minutes ago: "Yet another anti-pigs' feet article from this prejudiced rag. Shame on you, *Daily Complainer!*"

THE DAILY COMPLAINER

Wednesday, August 3

SAN FRANCISCO. In an exclusive interview, Ms. Amy McDougall told the *Daily Complainer* about her bizarre experiences today.

When Ms. McDougall emerged from her bedroom this morning, she found a sign in the hall reading HOY ES EL DÍA DE SOLO HABLAR ESPAÑOL. This means, "Today is the day of only speaking Spanish."

"Are you serious?" Ms. McDougall asked Mr. Diaz. Mr. Diaz is the McDougalls' house guest for three very long days running, with four more to go.

"*No entiendo,*" Mr. Diaz replied, which translates: "I don't understand." He repeated, "*Hoy es el día de solo hablar español.*"

Mr. Diaz asked Ms. McDougall, in Spanish, if it wasn't nice of him to arrange for this special day. Ms. McDougall would learn so much.

At first, Ms. McDougall was happy for an excuse not to speak to Mr. Diaz for an entire day. However, she soon found that if she spoke to her dad in English, Mr. Diaz would pop up, exclaiming "*¡No, no, no!*" They were only supposed to speak Spanish, he insisted.

Even when Ms. McDougall addressed her cat Flora, Mr. Diaz would swoop down with his "*¡No, no, no!*" Fortunately, Ms. McDougall has the ability to telepath with Flora, exchanging thoughts in no specific language.

Comments: 1

Grace Kwan, 13 minutes ago: "Why so many articles about that bubble-brained crybaby Amy McDougall? You call this news, *Daily Complainer?*"

THE DAILY COMPLAINER

Thursday, August 4

SAN FRANCISCO. The Society for the Prevention of Cruelty to Teenagers today revealed a particularly shocking case involving the McDougall family. To get the full story, our reporter interviewed the teen in question, Ms. Amy McDougall.

"My family has a long tradition of Movie Musical Nights," she explained. "That tradition was rudely interrupted this evening by our pest—I mean, guest, Mr. Enrique Diaz.

"In place of our beloved MMN, Mr. Diaz presented a slide show of his native Puerto Rico. He said the show would reveal to us the most beautiful places to visit if we ever went there.

"'My slide show will be just as fun as a musical,' Mr. Diaz assured us. Dozens of shots of tropical beaches, with slow zooming in and out, was certainly not as fun. It was more like 'fun' spelled backward. As in 'nuf.' As in 'enuf already.'

"To punish Mr. Diaz for mistreating me, the Society should strap him to a chair and force him to watch a seven-hour-long slide show I've made. It's called 'A Day in My Backyard, or Three Leaves Falling off a Tree and Some Ants Scurrying

Around, with Lots of Slow Zooming In and Out.'"

Comments: 1

Grace Kwan, 37 ½ minutes ago: "Enuf already, *Daily Complainer.*"

THE DAILY COMPLAINER

Friday, August 5

SAN FRANCISCO. Neighbors of the McDougalls reported an ominous calm in the area today. Our reporter contacted Ms. Amy McDougall inside the family home to find out more.

"It's spooky," Ms. McDougall told the *Daily Complainer* in a whisper. "I've hardly heard anything outside my bedroom all day, just a little rustling and tapping and what sounded like a balloon bursting. The few times I've left my room, I've found the living room door shut.

"—Oh, I can hear my dad getting home, returning from his photography studio. He's climbing the stairs. He's coming down the hall. He's opening the door to the living room—"

On the other end of the line, our reporter could hear people shout, "Surprise!" Ms. McDougall told him she would investigate. Returning a short time later, she said, "Our house guest has thrown a surprise party for me and my dad to celebrate his stay with us."

"So he invited all of your friends?" our reporter asked.

"No," Ms. McDougall said. "All his friends. He said he couldn't invite our friends without asking for their numbers and explaining why he wanted them, and then it wouldn't have been a surprise.

"I told Mr. Diaz I had a headache and didn't feel up to attending a party with a bunch of complete strangers. I remained in my room while the party rocked on into the late hours. My cat Flora stayed with me. She telepathed to Mr.

Diaz that she had a headache, too, though I'm not sure he received her message."

Comments: 1

Grace Kwan, 4 minutes ago: "Oh, please! This article isn't even worthy of some trashy middle school paper like the *Maroon Baboon*. I'm canceling my subscription—and don't you dare complain!"

Chapter 24

Saturday morning, Enrique loaded all his stuff back into Dad's car, ready to return to his own apartment. "I don't know how you guys feel," he said cheerfully, "but as far as I'm concerned, the trial week was a big success."

No one in my family said how they felt. Not me, not Dad, not Flora. Maybe we were all too wiped out by Enrique's visit. Once Dad got home after taking Enrique to his place, the three of us spent Saturday sprawled in different parts of the apartment, staring at the ceiling.

Sunday morning, Brian invited us to Woodside. "Edith and Grace and Denry are coming," he told Dad. "Of course, ask Enrique if he can join us too."

Unfortunately, he could.

Once we were there and sitting around the pool, Brian mentioned his redwood grove.

"You have a redwood grove?" Edith said. She was always interested in anything involving plants.

"It's only three trees," Brian said, "but I call it a grove. Come on, everyone. I'll show you."

Brian's property ran up a hillside, and the grove was tucked away in one of the far corners. As we headed up to it, Enrique shifted into school-teacher mode. I didn't have to worry I'd miss a single interesting thing because he was sure to point out all of them—a squirrel darting up a tree, a hawk circling overhead, a stinging nettle plant we shouldn't touch.

We reached the three redwood trees. Enrique patted the

shaggy reddish brown bark of one of them. "Who can tell me the age of the oldest redwood trees?"

"I can!" Denry exclaimed. Out went his chin, which meant he had something smart to say. "They're over two thousand years old."

"Very good, Denry. Can you tell me when redwoods first appeared on earth?"

"Two hundred and forty million years ago."

"Before dinosaurs or after?"

Denry bit his lower lip, thinking. "After dinosaurs, but before birds, and flowers, and spiders."

Enrique applauded. "That's right!"

"A gold star for Denry," I whispered to Grace.

She gazed at Denry with lovey-dovey eyes. "I love men who know lots of things."

Looking down the hillside, Dad said, "I think this is the prettiest spot on your whole property, Brian."

Edith sat down on the ground with her back to one of the trees. "Yes. It's so quiet. I grew up in Hong Kong, and I love living in a city. But I do enjoy getting out into the countryside like this once in a while."

Smiling down at her, Brian said, "Maybe someday I'll persuade you to change your priorities. Then you can live in the country and visit the city."

Edith chuckled. "I can be impulsive. You never know what I might do if someone made me the right offer."

Grace and I walked around to the other side of the trees, looking up at them. "What's this talk about living in the country?" I said, lowering my voice. "Is Brian trying to get Edith to move to Woodside?"

Grace shrugged. "It's just something they tease each other about. You know how people are when they're in love. They'd run out of things to say to each other if they didn't make up a lot of nonsense."

"'Oh, Denry,'" I said, imitating her. "'Tell me more about redwood trees. Everything you say is *so* interesting!'"

"Behave yourself," Grace said, "or I'll push you into some stinging nettles. And thanks to Enrique, I know exactly what they look like."

❧

"Now that you've seen my magnificent redwood grove, shall we go fire up the grill and have some lunch?" Brian asked, looking around at us.

Edith said, "I'll join you in a while. First I'm going to soak up some more of the peace and quiet."

I wasn't eager to be around Enrique more than necessary, so I said I'd stay there with Edith. "Grace, what about you?" I asked.

Grace looked at her mom and me, then at Denry. "I'm going to head back to the house. Maybe Denry and I can have a splash in the pool before lunch."

I cocked an eyebrow at Grace. I thought, *Gee, I find my best friend a boyfriend, and guess which one of us she wants to spend more time with.*

As the others walked away, I sat down near Edith on the brown carpet of redwood twigs.

"How did Enrique's visit go?" she asked. "Your dad hasn't said much about it to me."

I picked a twig off the ground and brushed it up and down my bare leg. "Well…"

I seesawed between giving some namby-pamby answer and telling the truth. I decided to go with the truth. "The fact is, his visit was absolutely, entirely, thoroughly awful."

"I'm so sorry to hear that, Amy."

"I dread having him live with us even longer after he moves

133

out of his apartment," I said. "And I know my dad. He's so soft-hearted. Once Enrique moves in, if he likes it there, Dad will let him stay forever."

Edith put her hand on my shoulder. "I understand it's hard for you to have someone added to the Amy and Travis world. It's been just the two of you for so long. It isn't always easy for Grace to have Brian added to our world."

In a flash of anger, I threw the twig away from me as hard as I could. "Enrique is like—like a bulldozer. He mows down everything in his path."

"Your dad seems very into him."

"He's just blinded by love."

"Oh yes, love." Edith sighed. "Life would be so much simpler if people never fell in love, wouldn't it? Tell me, do you not think Enrique and your dad are right for each other?"

I made up my mind then and there. "No, I don't. I think someone should find Dad a different boyfriend."

Edith gave me a puzzled look. "Why do you say someone should find him one? You talk as if he can't do it himself."

I'd almost let the secret of my matchmaking slip out. "I mean, he should find a person on his own, or someone else should find him one, or whatever it takes."

"Have you told your dad that?"

"No. He'd just say I'm only thirteen and don't know what I'm talking about." Suddenly I had an idea. "Why don't you tell him, Edith?"

She looked surprised. "Tell him he shouldn't be seeing Enrique?"

"Yeah. He'd listen to you."

"I wouldn't be so sure about that. Not if he's blinded by love." Edith stroked her chin a few times, as if she were thinking. "Amy, has Enrique ever been mean to you?"

"No, not exactly."

"Untrustworthy? Lying? Malicious?"

"Well, none of those things either," I admitted. "Not exactly."

Edith didn't say anything. Instead, she just looked at me, like she was waiting for me to say something.

At last, I said, "I think you're telling me I should just put up with Enrique."

"If Enrique is doing something that bothers you, you should deal with it. Talk to him, talk to your dad."

"But other than that, put up with him."

"What if you got a boyfriend you really, really liked, and your dad didn't? A boyfriend who wasn't exactly mean or untrustworthy or any of those other things, but that your dad just didn't get along with. What would you want him to do?"

I didn't bother saying the answer out loud: *Put up with him.*

Chapter 25

I thought lunch that day would never end.

Dad and Enrique talked on and on about what color Enrique should paint an old chest of drawers he'd bought at a garage sale, handing color chips back and forth. "How about Brookside Moss?" "Or maybe Saffron Sands?"

Edith and Brian talked on and on about how they could landscape Brian's property. "I'd love to put a gazebo at one end of the pool." "Or how about a fountain?"

Grace and Denry talked on and on about what college they wanted to attend. "I have my heart set on Cal." "But think how cool it would be to tell people you're going to Yale."

Looking from one of these couples to the other, I felt like the odd girl out. I wanted to sneak off and have some time on my own. But first Dad wanted to take some pictures of us lined up on one side of the pool, using the timer on his camera. "Just one more shot," he kept saying. One more, one more.

Finally, I slipped away to the big oak tree on the other side of the house. Hanging from a thick branch was a swing made from a board and two pieces of rope. I swung back and forth on it, my eyes closed. I wished I could go on swinging forever, feeling the warm air swoosh against my bare legs and arms.

Suddenly I heard quick footsteps crunching over the leaves toward me. "Amy, help!" I heard Grace call out.

"What's the matter?" I asked, opening my eyes.

Grace dropped on the ground in front of me. "My life is over!" she wailed.

"Did Denry break up with you?"

"No," Grace said. "We're still planning to attend a prestigious university together and get matching his-and-hers PhDs."

"What's happened then?"

Grace pressed the tips of her fingers against her temples, as if whatever her problem was, it had given her a terrible headache.

"Suddenly Brian has my mom all excited about the idea of moving in with him. He said, 'Imagine what it would be like to landscape these whole two acres and live here while you work on them.' Mom got this glazed, fanatical look in her eyes. She said, 'I could make this place a showcase.'"

"But isn't it nice for your mom that Brian wants her to live with him?" I asked. "It means he's serious about her." As a matchmaker, I was concerned about the happiness of the couples I brought together.

Grace scowled. "It may be nice for her, but not for me. They're saying I can live in the chicken coop."

"The chicken coop?"

"Actually, the storeroom, though with that horrible, dirty old chicken coop right next to it."

I chewed on a knuckle, thinking hard. "Tell your mom you can't move down here when you're just about to start school at Mission High. Say it would be 'disruptive.' That always scares parents off, to say something will be 'disruptive' for us kids."

Grace twisted her mouth angrily. "That might have worked—except for Denry."

As if drawn by the sound of his name, Denry strode up. "I was worried about you, rushing off like that," he said to Grace.

Grace stared up at him, her hands bunched into fists. "It might have worked, except Denry told Mom and Brian how great the move would be for me from an academic point of view. Denry said Woodside High was much better than Mission High. Denry said a lot of professors from Stanford University lived in Woodside, and they made sure their kids went to a first-rate school."

I frowned. "Denry, I just don't understand why you're so down on Mission High."

"I'm sorry," he said. "Mission may be an okay school, but it just isn't the best. Grace needs to go to a school like Lowell or Woodside. Not just for the teachers, but because she'll be surrounded by kids who challenge and motivate her."

I put my hands on my hips. "Not to get personal, Denry, but I am going to be one of Grace's fellow students at Mission High. Do you think I don't challenge and motivate her?"

About five words into this nine-word question, I realized I'd probably be sorry I asked it.

"Frankly, no," Denry shot back. "In my humble opinion, you're a bad influence on Grace. You're not serious about your studies or anything else. You're like so many other kids. You just want to drift along and have fun and not think about your future."

I jumped out of the swing and took a step toward Denry. He moved back, as if worried I'd punch him in the nose.

"Grace gets straight As," I said. "She's learning Mandarin. We were in the journalism club together at Everett. How can you say I or anyone else has been a bad influence on her? Grace is doing just fine."

Denry was like someone in danger of losing a fight who had no choice except to haul out his biggest weapon. "I have just one question for you, Amy McDougall. Why did Grace sign up at Mission High and not try to get into Lowell?"

"Well, because…" I stared at Grace. And she looked away. That meant…

"Grace," I said. "Are you going to Mission because I am? Because that's where I have to go?"

Grace cleaned her glasses on her shirttail. "A lot of factors went into my decision," she mumbled.

Grace still didn't look at me. As far as I was concerned, that revealed the truth. That, yes, she was mainly going to Mission High because I was, her best friend.

At home later, I sat at my desk playing with my Amy McDougall, Master Matchmaker business cards. Brian's company had sent me a hundred, and I still had ninety-nine left.

I tried to make a tower, the way people did with playing cards. I could get a few cards to stand up, leaning against each other. As soon as I tried to add another layer, they all collapsed.

Did I want Dad to break up with Enrique? Edith with Brian, for that matter, and Grace with Denry? For them to stop moving forward in life two by two and go back to one by one? I remembered what Edith had said: "Life would be simpler if people never fell in love." Had we been better off before silly old Love stuck his nose in our business?

If the couples broke up, I'd have to renounce my title of Master Matchmaker. Darn, and matchmaking was the one thing I was definitely better at than Grace.

Maybe I'd even be sacrificing the start of a brilliant career. I saw myself opening a matchmaking service, McDougall Matchmaking, Inc. I'd be interviewed on television and radio. I'd write a bunch of bestselling books about matchmaking. People would be so grateful to me. "Amy McDougall," I could hear them say, "you've made me the happiest person in the world!"

I tried to make a tower again. I cheated a little, using the side of my laptop to support one card.

And still the cards collapsed, making a sad little clatter.

Chapter 26

At first during the summer, I was sometimes flaky about crossing off the days on the wall calendar Grace had given me. I might not get around to it until the next morning, or even the next evening. Now that the calendar showed the Chinese symbol for August, every night before going to bed, I itched to take my black marker and make a very thick, very dark X on the day that had just ended.

Each day that I crossed out brought me closer to the end of this crazy summer, when I'd played matchmaker for other people and confusion-maker for myself. Each crossed-out day brought me nearer to the start of high school and an exciting new chapter in my life.

In honor of the super important change from "middle" to "high," I wanted to watch *High School Musical* with Dad on Movie Musical Night. We'd managed to keep MMN going through the summer. Sometimes Enrique tried to get himself invited or at least change the day. Usually Dad and I managed to fend him off.

Usually.

A cousin of Enrique's from Puerto Rico was passing through San Francisco. He was a big wine fan, and he wanted Enrique and Dad to go out with him to some famous wine bar. The only day he could meet them was the last Thursday of my summer vacation.

At least Enrique gave me a potted geranium as a way of apologizing. "I know it means a lot to you and your dad to have that time together," he told me.

Just as I was thinking that that was a nice thing to say, he added, "But you know in my culture, we don't believe it's so important to do lots of things by ourselves or with just one other person. We're more sociable."

All I said in response was, "Thanks for the geranium."

Since Dad wasn't available, I invited Grace and Edith over to watch the movie with me. I thought it would get both Grace and me even more excited about starting high school than we already were.

Except as I watched it, I kept asking myself, *But which high school is this movie showing, with all these kids who are mostly bright and motivated and even know how to sing and dance? Mission High or some snazzy school like Lowell or Woodside?*

I thought about the Mission High versus Lowell/Woodside business, and maybe Grace did too. We didn't discuss it, though. What was there to say at this point? We were hurtling forward on a rocket ship that would reach Planet Mission High in just a few days. There was no turning back.

Grace and Edith left soon after Dad and Enrique got home. I pretended to go to bed. In fact, I stayed up making sketches of Grace and me appearing in different numbers from the musical. I was especially proud of a drawing of us doing the splits five feet in the air.

I planned to give Grace the drawings as a way of saying, *I'm sorry if I've screwed up your life.*

I'd put too much salt on the popcorn we ate during the movie and wanted a glass of water. After listening at my door, I opened it a crack and peeked down the hall. I could hear Dad and Enrique talking in the living room. Good, that gave me a chance to sneak into the kitchen.

I was about to slip back into my room with my water when I caught a word in the guys' conversation: "Amy." I stood still. A short while later, I heard it again: "Amy."

I tiptoed into the dining room and hid near the arched entrance to the living room. I respected people's privacy—except when they were talking about me.

"It's not too late," I heard Enrique say. "I talked with Ms. Alberola at Mission High, and she said we could still get Amy into the class."

My face flushed, my heart thumped. I was holding the glass of water with my right hand. With my left, I took hold of a lock of my hair and twirled it furiously. I knew what Dad and Enrique were talking about: Accelerated Spanish. That was a special class with a tougher workload than regular Spanish.

"I appreciate your looking into that, Enrique," Dad said. "But I've already suggested to Amy a couple of times that she take the class, and I don't want to bring it up again. She had some good arguments against the idea. This is her first year in high school, and she's got tough subjects like geometry to deal with."

"I grew up in a family that spoke both English and Spanish," Enrique said, "and I'm so grateful for that. With every year that passes, though, it becomes harder for someone to learn a language."

"Well then, so Amy doesn't learn Spanish as fast. Perhaps years from now she'll be sorry. I think that's better than my strong-arming her into something she really doesn't want to do."

"You give Amy too much decision-making power. Does a thirteen-year-old know it's a good idea for her to study something difficult like chemistry or Latin?"

"It's a balancing act, isn't it? A parent wants to push but not too much."

"I can tell you, you should be pushing more with Amy. I've had her in class, and I've spent a lot of time with her on the courts. She's a great kid but not a self-starter. If left to her own devices, she just fritters away most of her time."

"She has been taking tennis lessons."

"Yes, though frankly she doesn't seem very enthusiastic about them. If I hadn't heard her ask to go to a tennis summer camp, I wouldn't have thought she had much interest in the game."

"You said she's doing pretty well, though."

"She is. Still, she won't become a really strong player until she has some fire in the belly."

I heard a sound like one of the guys standing up. I darted back to my room with my glass of water, worried they'd catch me eavesdropping on them.

I hardly slept that night. I was too busy tossing and turning and being furious with Enrique.

I flipped over on my stomach. How dare Enrique say that I wasn't a self-starter. And that I didn't have "a fire in my belly." Even though I wasn't exactly sure what that was, his saying I didn't have it made me mad.

I spun around onto my back. And that was the thanks I got for playing Cupid with Enrique and Dad, to have him badmouth me.

I flopped onto my side. Enrique Diaz had better watch his step. I'd brought Dad and him together, and I could break them up if I wanted. I was Amy McDougall, Master Matchmaker. And Master Match-Unmaker, too!

The next day, I met Enrique at Everett for my last tennis lesson. I was still bubbling with anger. All I could focus on was not saying something rude to him. If I could just get through these two hours, I'd be almost at the weekend. After that would come scary-exciting Monday and my first day at Mission High. Then I'd have tons of more important things to think about than Mr. Enrique Diaz.

In today's lesson, Enrique fixated on my serve.

"If you don't serve well," he called to me from across the

court, "no matter how good you are at other things, you aren't going to win any games."

Balls were flying over the net. So were Enrique's criticisms. "You're not on balance when you serve, Amy. You're throwing the ball too high. You aren't hitting the ball at the top of the toss."

My lips hurt from pinching them together so much. I kept telling myself: *I won't lose my temper, I won't tell him to shut up, I won't say something like, What do you expect from a non-starter like me?*

Finally the lesson ended. Enrique and I dropped down onto the bench next to the court to cool off. I chugged some water from my bottle. He wiped his face with a towel. Neither of us said anything. That felt awkward.

At last, I came out with, "Well, thanks a lot for all these lessons."

"We should try to keep them going during the school year," Enrique said. "Maybe on Saturday or Sunday afternoon."

I didn't know how to respond. I couldn't just say what I thought, which was that I'd rather be left in the desert with my hands and feet tied to stakes and surrounded by tarantulas and rattlesnakes.

Instead I said, "I appreciate your giving me so much of your time."

Enrique said, "If I give you some of my time, that makes me feel better about taking away some time you might spend with your dad. This weekend, for example."

I sat up straighter, puzzled. "This weekend? What about it?"

"I'm going to try to persuade your dad to run away with me to Mendocino for a romantic weekend. After all, it's my last one before I jump back into work."

My face suddenly felt hot, my mouth dry. "But it's my last weekend too. The last one before I start high school."

I emphasized "high school," to show how it must be more

important than anything to do with Enrique's dumb adult life.

"Was there something special you wanted to do?" Enrique asked.

"Yeah. Spend time with my dad. That's special to me."

"You'd like him to stay home so you two can just sit around the apartment?"

I forced myself to come up with some sort of plan. "Maybe the three of us can go out to dinner."

We'd already done this a bunch of times, so my plan didn't sound very exciting.

"Actually," I went on, "Dad told me he thinks you guys are spending too much time together."

While I said this, I didn't look at Enrique, instead I stared at the metal pole holding up one end of the net. It was easier to lie if I wasn't looking at him.

My lie worked in the moment. It meant I wasn't criticizing an adult. Instead, I was only repeating what Dad had (supposedly) said to me.

Enrique had been running his hand through his thick black hair. When I told my lie, his hand stopped about halfway back. "Your dad thinks we're spending too much time together? He never told me that."

My heartbeat picked up its pace. It said, *Go on, go on, do it, do it, say it, say it!*

"You know my dad. He keeps a lot to himself."

"He's keeping things to himself?"

The snowball picked up more snow as it rolled down the hill, getting bigger.

"You know, things like thinking you're kind of—" I was about to say "a bossy-pants," but that wasn't a Dad word. I struggled to come up with something more appropriate. "Kind of domineering."

"Domineering?"

"Yeah. Like when he wants to do something, and you want to do something else, the two of you always end up doing what you want. Or like when he says he thinks such-and-such, and you don't just say you have a different opinion. You say, 'No, this is how it is.'"

I waited for Enrique to respond. When he didn't, I turned and looked at him. His mouth was folded down at the corners. His brown eyes looked wet, as if he might cry.

I tried to backpedal. "I—Dad doesn't necessarily mean domineering in a bad way. Actually, he likes that you're a boss—a take-charge type. For instance, when you organized that Bowling and Banana Splits Night for all of us on Monday—"

"I know, I know. I should have checked to make sure the bowling alley was open then."

The snowball was careening down the mountain, out of my control.

"We ended up having a fun evening, though," I said. "So what if it was Banana Splits and No Bowling Night?"

"Your dad kept giving me a hard time. Talking about how we were taking in lots of calories without burning any."

"He was just kidding, Enrique. You know my dad. He's a big kidder."

Enrique stood up. "I need to get going, Amy. Thanks for telling me things I didn't know about how your dad sees our relationship." He managed a crooked smile. "That's something I like about kids your age. You're often better at just laying things on the line."

I watched Enrique walk across the school yard. He didn't look around, so he didn't see that I had my hands pressed against my cheeks in an oh-my-God-what-have-I-done? expression.

Chapter 27

"Way way way way bad." That was Grace's reaction when I called her later and told her what I'd done.

"Okay, okay, it was bad." I was in my room, sitting at my desk. "Enrique will tell Dad what I told him. Dad will get mad at me, and I'll have to apologize. Then the whole thing will blow over."

"Since we're on the phone and you can't see me, I'm telling you that I'm rolling my eyes. As in, 'You don't get how serious this is, do you?'"

Restless, I put Grace on speaker, stood up, and started moving around my scented candles on the shelves above my desk. Instead of ordering them alphabetically, maybe it would be a fun change to arrange them by color.

I told Grace, "I said what I said, and I can't take it back. What am I supposed to do now?"

"For a start, stop telling Enrique your dad thinks he's domineering."

"But he is, and maybe someone needed to call him on that."

"It's not your business, Amy Baby."

I took a big whiff of my current favorite candle, wild cranberry. I hoped it would make me feel better. It didn't.

"Sometimes I think it was a mistake for me to get Dad and Enrique together," I said. "Maybe I can find someone who's better for Dad. I'm sure my matchmaking skills have improved now that I've had more experience."

"Finding your dad a different boyfriend isn't your business

either, you numbskull. He seems to like the one he already has."

After I ended my call with Grace, Flora sauntered in from the hall. She sat at my feet and stared up at me. She telepathed, *I don't approve of what you did either.*

"Who asked you?" I yelled. Flora scampered out of the room.

I waited for Dad to get home. Once he did, I looked for signs that Enrique had called him and that I was in hot water. I couldn't find any. Dad was in a good mood. He'd just gotten an assignment to take the photos for an Italian cookbook.

"I'll see if I can bring home some of the food after I take pictures of it," he joked.

Over dinner, Dad asked if I'd had a good last lesson with Enrique. Here was my opening to say, *Dad, I have something to confess,* and tell him the whole shocking story. Instead, I mumbled, "Yeah, sure."

"Now that Enrique has turned you into a champion tennis player, I want him to give me some lessons too."

I made a vague sound through a mouthful of fried zucchini and onions.

"Would you recommend him as a coach?"

I grabbed my glass of water and took a drink to excuse my not saying anything. Instead, I just nodded.

I was thinking about making a vow to speak as little as possible for the rest of my life. Didn't most of my problems start when I opened my big mouth and let words come out? It might be better if I never opened it, except when I had something absolutely essential to say. Like, "The apartment is on fire." Or, "That man has a gun pointed at you."

"Is there anything special you want to do on the last weekend of your summer vacation?" Dad asked.

I was terrified Dad would suggest we do something with

Enrique. Enrique was the last person I wanted to see right now.

I said, "I'm worried this first week at school may be stressful. So I think I'd rather just have a quiet weekend at home."

❧

I got my wish for a quiet weekend. It was so quiet that the quiet got on my nerves. I kept waiting for Enrique to call. Dad was waiting too. He checked his phone every fifteen minutes.

"That's strange," Dad said. "I've left a message for Enrique and sent him a couple of texts, but he hasn't responded."

"He's probably just busy," I said.

I hoped that was the reason.

Chapter 28

Monday, most of my brain cells were busy with other things, and I didn't have many left for thinking about Dad and Enrique.

In the morning, the first question was what to wear. One of Grace's cousins who was a senior had told us that what we wore on the first day of high school was super important. "However people see you then is the way they'll see you for the rest of the school year," she said.

I tried on all my favorite clothes and studied myself in my full-length mirror. In the end, I combined my lacy white top with my turquoise skinny jeans. The top said, *I'm basically a nice quiet girl.* The jeans added, *But I also have a fun side.*

To get to Mission High, I had to walk past Everett, which was only a block away from it. I waved hello to my old school as I passed. Looking at the brick steps leading to the entrance, I thought, *Thank goodness I'll never have to climb those again.*

When I reached Mission High, I stood gazing up at it from the far edge of the sidewalk. The building was bigger than Everett and had a cool-looking tower topped by a dome of shiny-colored tiles. It was hard to believe I'd be going to school here for the next four years. What would happen to me in all that time?

Well, Amy McDougall, I told myself, *there's only one way to find out, and that's to join all these other kids walking through the front doors.* So I did.

As I navigated the school, I worried some upperclassman would tease me or dump me in a trash can. Nothing like that happened. In fact, between second and third periods when I was looking for my English class, one older guy helped me find it.

Swirled in with lots of new faces were a bunch of ones I recognized from Everett. Some people I was glad to see again. Others I wasn't. Like Debbie Parado, who turned away when she spotted me. I gathered she still wasn't speaking to me, for who knew what reason.

What if Debbie and I went to the same college and were assigned to be roommates? Would she still not talk to me? Assuming a slow-starting, bad-influencing girl like me actually managed to go to college.

Grace and I spent the entire lunch hour gabbing about our new classes. Mainly this was fun. Except for a few times when we almost ran smack into the Subject We Weren't Discussing.

"I'm so glad we're taking world history together," Grace said. "Most of the other kids in that class are such lamebrains. I mean, really, Mr. Wright had to call on five people to show where Syria was on the map before he got to me. I'm sure that wouldn't happen at—"

Later, she said, "Algebra II looks like it's going to be easier than I thought. I want to ask Denry if he's using the same textbook at—"

Later still, "It's stupid my counselor won't let me take trig this year too. I bet they'd let me at—"

Each time Grace broke off a sentence like that, I wanted to yell, "Go ahead and say it, 'at Lowell, at Lowell, at Lowell'! I know, everything would be better if only you were going to Lowell."

Donna Rodriguez was one of the Everett people I was glad to see. She was in my last class of the day. I ended up going to her home afterward. I stayed for a couple of hours while we talked about our summers, and whether black nail polish was still cool, and things like that.

When I got home, I found Dad in the living room standing in front of his shelves of CDs. He gave me a hug. Dad was a good hugger. He made his hugs long and almost too strong, though not quite.

"How was your first day at school, sweet potato?" he asked.

"Not too bad," I said.

"It looks like you're still in one piece."

"Yep, I am." I held out my arms, then my legs, first my right, then my left.

"I want to hear all about it. Every last detail."

We sat together on the couch. I didn't tell Dad all the details, but a lot. At last I said, "What were you doing when I came in?"

"Alphabetizing our CDs of musicals. I've been meaning to do this for weeks, and at last I'm taking the time." Dad went back to the shelves. "What do you think, should *All That Jazz* come before *Allegro* or after?"

"It doesn't matter, as long as they're close to each other. The important thing is that you can find them when you want."

"Wow, Amy pie! Today was only your first day in high school, and already you're so intelligent."

While Dad moved around some more CDs, I played with my hair. I wondered if I should pile it on top of my head tomorrow or pull it back in a ponytail. What image did I want to get across?

After a minute, Dad said, "We never did turn Enrique into a fan of musicals, did we?"

I froze with my hands in my hair. "No. I guess not."

"It's odd I still haven't heard from him." Dad used his fingernail to scratch a price tag off the cover of a used CD. "I hope nothing has happened to him."

I put my hands in my lap. I looked at Dad's back as he stood there. He was wearing the brown sweater I liked, the pullover one with a collar. "I'm sure nothing has."

Nothing except my telling him he was an awful person.

Dad gave a sad laugh. "I also hope he isn't giving me the brush-off."

"That can't be it." I bit the knuckle of my thumb, trying to come up with something else to say. "Enrique likes you."

"Do you think so? If he is giving me the brush-off, I wish he'd tell me. You know, call and say, 'I'm brushing you off. Have a nice day.'"

"He's probably just busy." That excuse was getting lame.

"Is anyone too busy to send a one-sentence text saying he's busy? During three days plus?" Dad looked at me over his shoulder. "I'll tell you who's someone Enrique likes. You."

"Me?" I could feel my eyes get wide with surprise.

"He thinks you're very smart, for one thing. That's why it bothers him when you don't give your hundred percent to something."

I was so confused by now. I didn't know whether to twirl my hair or bite my knuckle.

Dad went on, "We'd have had a pretty dull summer without him, don't you think? No tennis lessons, no bowling night without the bowling. Speaking of the summer, I've got some prints to show you of the pictures I took at Brian's last pool party."

A minute ago, if someone had asked me whether I'd enjoyed that party, I'd have said no. In the photos, on the other hand, all of us looked like we were having a great time. What was the truth?

The photo I spent the most time looking at showed the seven of us standing along one side of the pool. Dad had set a timer so he could join us in the shot.

Grace suddenly got it into her head that this would be a much better picture if it caught someone falling into the pool, namely me. She tried to shove me forward with one hand on my back, and I resisted. Still, caught off guard, I might have fallen in—except that Enrique, standing beside me, held me firmly by the shoulders.

The whole business was over in a few seconds, and I forgot about it. But the camera had caught it. Grace pushing, me struggling, Enrique holding on. Somehow he'd known in a snap of the fingers that I didn't want to get pushed into the pool, that I wouldn't have thought that was fun and funny. So he'd kept it from happening.

Dad was missing Enrique. And I had to admit—I was missing him a little too.

Chapter 29

Grace and I had lunch together again on our second day at Mission High. This time, gabbing about school only got us through me eating my egg salad sandwich and Grace eating her kung pao chicken. We had time to talk about other things—like Enrique.

"What's happening with that?" Grace asked. "Are you in big trouble with your dad?"

"What's happening is that nothing is happening," I said. "Enrique just isn't responding to Dad. Which kind of solves the problem."

Grace frowned. "Whose problem?"

"My problem. Enrique fades away, and Dad never knows what I did. Then maybe I find Dad someone else to date, or else he finds someone on his own."

"Wait a minute," Grace said, throwing up her hands. "That isn't a solution, for Enrique to believe something that isn't true and break up with your dad because of it. Shouldn't you be acting more mature?"

"How?" As soon as I asked this, I was sorry. I was sure the how would involve me doing something I didn't want to.

"Isn't it obvious? You go to Enrique and tell him what you did. You grovel and hope he forgives you. But most of all you hope he gets in touch with your dad."

"You want me to tell Enrique that I'm a complete liar?"

"Yeah. And you know where to find him. At Everett."

I shook my head, looking at the ground. "I can't do it."

"You can. You just don't want to. But if you don't do it, I'll never speak to you again."

"You aren't serious?" I thought of Debbie Parado. She was managing never to speak to me again, and with her, I didn't even know why.

"I might speak to you a little, though only to call you names, like blockhead and nitwit. Your dad is a nice guy, and he deserves to be treated nicely."

The bell rang, telling us it was time to head to our classes. Grace wiped her mouth with a napkin. "Did I get off all my kung pao chicken?"

"Yeah. What about me? Do I look okay?"

Grace and I had agreed to keep an eye on each other's appearance now that we were in high school. We didn't want to talk to some senior, then find later we had a booger hanging from our nose.

Grace looked me over critically. "You've got something sticking out of your shirt pocket."

She plucked out a strip of pink paper and handed it to me. It was a fortune from a fortune cookie. Probably one of many I'd gotten from Edith at her dinners.

"Thanks." Without bothering to read the fortune, I stuck it in my geometry textbook and hurried across the courtyard toward the entrance.

Geometry was my first class in the afternoon. While waiting for the rest of the kids to arrive, I flipped open my textbook. I turned some pages to see if anything in it made sense. I came to the page where I'd stuck the fortune.

I took it out and read it. The fortune said, *If you have something good in your life, don't let it go.*

Now I remembered. That was the fortune I'd gotten the night I had the idea of finding Edith a boyfriend. I must have stuck it in the pocket of this shirt and forgotten about it. Since the shirt was pink and the paper was pink, I hadn't noticed it while getting dressed this morning.

Except it hadn't really been my fortune, had it? It had been Enrique's. And what had mine been, the one I should have gotten? I remembered I hadn't let Enrique read it to me, beyond the word *Don't.*

Mr. Vining started the class. I had trouble concentrating on what he said about line segments and end points. I kept thinking about my talk with Grace. Was she right? Could I not just hide my head in the sand? Did I have to find Enrique and tell him the horrible, embarrassing truth?

I thought of Dad yesterday. Dad in his brown sweater that I liked. How he'd seemed sad because Enrique had disappeared. Dad had done so much for me. I had to try to clean up this mess, for his sake.

"Darn that Grace!" I muttered half out loud. "She is right, as usual."

Chapter 30

I was supposed to meet Grace after school and go to her place. She was waiting for me at the main entrance.

The first thing I said to her was, "Will you go to Everett with me?"

"Why?"

"For moral support."

Grace pushed her glasses up her nose. "Okay."

We walked to Everett. It was a nice sunny day. Too nice a day for me to be about to do something totally humiliating.

We climbed the brick steps to the entrance. The steps that yesterday I'd told myself I'd never have to walk up again. We passed through one of the doors with the pretty tiles around them.

I expected the security guard to challenge us. "What are you two doing here?" he would say. "It's obvious you're much too old to be middle school students." Instead, all he did was glance at us, then look back at his phone.

We walked past the rows of bright yellow lockers, along the shiny yellow floor, between the daisy-petal yellow walls. Through all that yellowness that I'd also been happy to think I'd never see again.

Nearing the door to Enrique's classroom, I could see that it was open. I stopped a few yards away. I felt Grace take my hand and squeeze it. I turned to her.

"Good luck," she whispered.

"Thanks, Gracie." I smiled at her, then moved toward the door.

Maybe Enrique wasn't in this room. Maybe the administration had moved teachers around since last year. But, no, once I was in the doorway, I could see him sitting at his desk, writing something. I'd moved quietly, so he hadn't heard me.

I looked back at Grace. She made a *Go on* gesture with one hand.

I wasn't sure what to do. I knocked three times on the door, though it was open. Enrique looked over at me. Suddenly I remembered that, here at Everett, he was Mr. Diaz again, not Enrique.

Feeling like an idiot, I raised my hand and waved. "Hi," I said.

"Hi, Amy," Enrique said. He was just looking at me. He didn't have any particular expression on his face. "What brings you here?"

Grace had told me I should grovel. I remembered seeing a movie set during the Middle Ages where a woman groveled in front of a king. She lay right down on her stomach on the floor and stretched her hands in front of her and said, "Forgive me, sire!" Was that what I was supposed to do?

I took a few more steps into the room. I couldn't say what I had to say from the doorway.

I cleared my throat. Then I got right to the point.

"Last Friday, after our tennis lesson, I told you a bunch of things that weren't true."

Up shot Enrique's black eyebrows. "Oh?"

"Everything I said about—well, about you, that was all made up. Completely. My dad never said any of those things."

"Oh?" Enrique repeated. He seemed to think over what I'd told him. Then he nodded a few times. "Okay, so those were not things your dad said?"

"No."

"None of them?"

"No. My dad has never said anything bad about you to me."

"I'm glad you told me that, Amy. It makes a difference."

Enrique folded his hands in front of him. I tensed. That wasn't a good sign, when teachers folded their hands. Usually they did that before they said I had detention or they were giving me an F on a test.

"But they weren't completely invented, were they?" Enrique said.

"How do you mean?"

"I mean that someone did say them. You."

I opened my mouth, then closed it again. "Well…"

"You think those things are true about me, don't you? That I'm—what did you say? Domineering?"

I looked away from Enrique, at the last row of student desks. Did I not only have to admit that my dad hadn't said them, but that I thought they were true?

"I was kind of mad at the time."

Enrique nodded, as if this was enough of an answer.

"I guess it's a fact that sometimes I can be domineering," he said. "My mom's nickname for me as a kid was El Principito, the Little Prince. She called me that because I was always telling my friends what to do, the way a prince would."

"Grace calls me…" I stopped.

"What?"

I could feel the blood rush into my face. "Bossy-pants. She says I try to tell people what to do all the time."

Enrique smiled slightly. "Perhaps you and I have some things in common." He tapped the pen he was holding on his desk a few times. "What do you think we should do about this situation, Amy?"

"First, I want to apologize."

"I accept your apology. What next, Miss Bossy-pants?"

I stared at Enrique. It seemed like he was giving me a chance to make a suggestion, not just get yelled at.

"Can you not say anything about this to my dad?" I asked.

"Wouldn't it be better if you told him the truth? I know that will be hard. But it was probably hard for you to tell me, too, and you've survived that."

My gaze returned to the last row of desks. "Well..."

"Think it over," Enrique advised.

I took a step back. I was dying to get out of that room. Still, I realized there was something else I should say.

"Can you call my dad? He's been wondering why you haven't."

"Do you want me to?"

"Yeah."

"You think your dad and I are a good match?"

Amy McDougall, Master Matchmaker, gulped some air. "I do," I said. I added to myself: *I thought you two were a good match before either of you did, though I admit I've had some doubts along the way.*

Then I remembered the fortune. I'd stuck it back in my geometry book. I pulled it out and gave it to him.

"What's this?" Enrique asked.

"Remember that time Edith had us to dinner, and I asked if someone would swap fortunes with me, and you said you would? That's the fortune you gave me. Now I think I shouldn't have interfered and that actually that fortune was meant for you."

Enrique read aloud, "'If you have something good in your life, don't let it go.'" He looked at me and smiled. His smile was bigger now and more relaxed. More like the smile of the Enrique I was used to.

"Thank you, Amy. It isn't actually a fortune, is it? More like advice. Advice from an advice cookie. Still, it's pretty good advice."

Enrique snapped his fingers, like he'd just recalled something.

He took a plastic bag out of one of his desk drawers, dumped the cards and flyers and bits of paper in it on the desk, and looked through them.

"As a teacher, I save all sorts of weird things like Chinese cookie fortunes. I never know what I might need in a lesson or to make a display. Ah! Here it is."

Enrique handed me a strip of paper. This one was white. He said, "I think this was your fortune."

I read, "'Don't fear change. It can lead to something better.'"

I was glad to have the fortune that should have been mine. I said goodbye to Enrique.

I rushed back to Grace where she waited in the hall, leaning against one of the day-glo lockers. I put my arm through hers and hustled her down the hall.

"How did it go?" she said.

"Great! I explained that the whole thing was your fault. I told Enrique you cast a spell on me and turned me into a zombie, and I was only following your wicked orders."

Grace whacked me on the arm, laughing.

After leaving Grace's, I got home at five-thirty. Dad wasn't there yet. I flopped down at one end the couch. Flora was at the other end, lying on her side. She basked in the sunlight pouring in through the bay window. Her legs with their white paws were all stuck out in the same direction. Her jade-green eyes were half closed.

I took the fortune out of my geometry book and studied it. The fortune that was definitely mine. The one on white paper, not pink.

I scratched Flora behind her ears. I telepathed to her, *Don't fear change. It can lead to something better. That means that if you get a boy-cat-friend or a girl-cat-friend, I should be glad and try to see the good things about the change.*

Flora looked at me through the parts of her eyes that were open. She communicated, *In the first place, I prefer being single. In the second place, I'm a cat, and I don't like change. If you made me move somewhere else with you or gave me to a different owner, I would not be amused.*

At that moment, I heard the street door close below, then Dad coming up the stairs. He was taking them two at a time. That was always a sign he was happy. And I couldn't think of any reason for his being especially happy today except that Enrique had called him.

Chapter 31

"Everything seems fine between us," Dad said cheerfully. "I did ask why he'd disappeared that way. All he said was it didn't have anything to do with me."

I took a breath in, let it out. I might as well take the plunge, I thought, and get it over with.

"Dad, I have something to tell you."

But Dad was already moving down the hall toward the kitchen. "Can we talk about it while we make dinner? I'm starving. I thought we'd have lemon chicken again. That's a quickie."

Part of me thought, *I can't say what I have to say while we make lemon chicken. I need your full attention.* Another part thought, *Actually, this may be easier if you're only half paying attention.*

As we worked on dinner, I got to the part of the story where I passed off my ideas about Enrique as Dad's. Dad stopped slicing a lemon and put a hand to his forehead. "Oh, Amy," he sighed.

Dad sounded disappointed. Nothing was worse than Dad being disappointed with me. I would rather have had him send me to my room without dinner or ground me for a week.

Later, the situation improved. "I'm proud of you for that," Dad said when I told him about admitting to Enrique what I'd done.

While I was telling Dad about my troubles, I threw in that Grace was upset that Edith was thinking about moving to Woodside. Also, for good measure, Denry saying I was a bad influence on Grace and Grace signing up for Mission High mainly because I was going there.

Dad paused while chopping parsley. Finally, he said, "I'm having second thoughts about Enrique living with us while his building gets fixed up. I don't think you're ready for that, and frankly I'm not sure I am either."

My mouth fell open. "Where will he go then?"

"Edith and I have been talking about this idea of her moving in with Brian. Of course, they're adults and can do whatever they like. But I'm going to suggest they wait a while. After all, they've only known each other a couple of months."

I twirled a lock of my hair, taking this in. "Okay."

"And if Edith doesn't move to Woodside, maybe Enrique can while he's out of his apartment. He loves Brian's place, and they get along well. We can all help fix up the storeroom for him."

"You said before he couldn't live there without a car."

"He can't. So he can borrow mine."

I thought what my fortune had said about not fearing change. Dad sure didn't seem afraid of it. He was making changes so fast, I had trouble following them all.

"You need it, though," I said.

"I can manage for a while. Use public transportation. Really, a lot of the time a car is only a headache in the city. Would you mind if we took a bus to Sophia's office?"

"No," I said, "I guess not."

"Now as for Denry and his attitude toward you…"

I clapped my hands to my face. "Dad, you're like a fairy godmother! Solving everyone's problems one right after another."

Dad chuckled. "A fairy god-dad."

"Still, I don't see what you can do about Denry and Grace and which high school she should go to and all that mess."

Dad stopped poking at the chicken breasts sizzling in the pan. He turned and fixed his blue eyes on me.

"My idea isn't that I'll do something. You will, Amy

McDougall. You'll prove to Denry he's wrong about you. You'll get your grades up at Mission High. If possible, you'll get straight As, like Grace."

Dad was pushing for yet another change, leaving me a little breathless. "You want me to get straight As? In classes like geometry?"

Looking back at the chicken breasts, Dad flipped them over. "In a way, Grace is the one who's been a bad influence. You've always let her be the smart one in the pair. You need to change that and make her share the role."

"Any other minor thing you want me to do besides get straight As?" I said, a little put out.

"I'm not sure. Maybe both you and Grace should apply for Lowell next year—provided you start knuckling down. We'll see how things go."

I laughed, shaking my head. "Dad, you're amazing!"

He raised his eyebrows. "Any other problems you want me to solve while I'm at it, Princess Ariel? Shall I find a boyfriend for you? I bet I'm pretty good at making matches."

At this, I jumped as if someone had stuck a needle in my arm. "Oh no!" I exclaimed. "One of those in the family is enough."

"How do you mean?"

"I mean, one match is enough, between you and Enrique."

Dad looked at me like he suspected that, for all the things I'd just told him, I'd left out something important.

Luckily for me, Dad was in a hurry to get dinner on the table and didn't ask any more questions.

The first thing I did after dinner was go to my room and call Grace. Once I'd told her about my talk with Dad, she said: "For heaven's sake, no more matchmaking, okay? The matches you've made so far have turned out well in the end. But next time you might not be so lucky. You might make some match that would completely blow up in your face."

"You're right, Gracie," I said, nodding. "Absolutely right."

"You'd better throw away those darned business cards."

"Excellent idea."

"Getting rid of them will remind you that you aren't a 'master matchmaker' anymore."

"I'll do it right now."

I opened a drawer in my desk and took out the box containing all ninety-nine cards. Then I hesitated, my hand suspended above my metal trash basket. I couldn't make my fingers open and let go of the box.

On the other end of the line, Grace asked, "Have you tossed them in the trash yet?"

"Yeah," I said.

"I didn't hear a plunk."

I stared into the completely empty trash basket. "That's because there was already a bunch of paper in the bottom."

"And you promise, no more matchmaking?"

"Yeah, yeah, yeah, sure, of course."

Talking to Grace about school stuff to cover up any suspicious sounds, I slipped the box back into the drawer, then very slowly and carefully closed it.